"We loved your story. When can we get more?" said a previous shuttle-taxi customer at the Fairbanks Airport.

"Man I read your manuscript. It was great! I want to read more, when is the book coming out?" said another returning passenger at the airport.

"I was reading the story and I forgot where I was sitting, and didn't notice the sounds around me. I was in the story. This guy that's got something, but doesn't know it! It's just a neat story really. He stumbles into fame with his homegrown ability. It really put my imagination to work and it fascinated me, even though I didn't really care about boxing." said Wisconsin photographer Andrew Fritz

Another reader gave the following written reply to the author:

"The mark of a good writer is his ability to form complete pictures in the mind of his readers. The mark of a terrific writer is his ability to form emotions in the heart of the reader. You are performing both tasks in this, while building goals + challenges for the primary character. These first three chapters captured me." - Cessna pilot Robert Grediagin

Another reader wrote the following email response:

"Talking with you at Deb's cafe in Fairbanks & reading your 15 pages of Champion was really interesting. Your method of crafting your words to paper to draw pictures in the readers mind is a real talent! Your life of working at so many jobs allows you the down to earth understanding of the common man's struggles of everyday life. Your quick precise mind (of minor details), allows a clear and picture ability to the reader of your story! I'm looking forward to your Bookssssssss! I have given your handout to my wife, she hasn't read it yet but I am sure she will enjoy it. Looking forward to seeing you again and reading your books! Don't let anything stand in your way; follow your dream & ability! You're a winner. Send your scripts to Hollywood it will be your Gold Mine in life."

-Trucker, Glen

***

CHAMPION

A Story of the Happy Life of Roman Lefthanded Losinski

Miles Cobbett

MC PUBLISHING

CONTENTS

To Bryan, Vera, John, Raymond and Geoffrey for doing all that you did and for knowing I had this book in me before I did and for understanding my need to touch the stove even after you've told me it's hot.

"The general desirous of winning a battle makes many calculations in his temple beforehand."

Sun Tsu, Chinese general 500 B.C.

Great love defies even death

ONE

Hey…what about my money?

The desert air was clear and crisp, at the boxing camp of former heavyweight champ Frank L. Jackson, when Roman Lefthanded Losinski appeared.

Roman had answered a help-wanted ad in the Sedona Times Courier, for a gardener's helper. As usual, the ad promised ten dollars-an-hour for labor work, but when Roman showed up to claim the job, he was informed that there was an 'error' by the newspaper and the most that he would be paid was eight dollars-an-hour (before deductions). He could have Sundays off, and working hours would be from 7 a.m. - 4 p.m. with a thirty-minute lunch. He could stay in the bunkhouse if needed, but it would cost him an extra twenty dollars-a-day, to be subtracted from his first paycheck.

The first days work was easy, mostly digging holes and putting in potted plants. His supervisor, an old Japanese gardener, took an instant liking to Roman and showed him where he could get water from a hose near the action of the boxing ring.

Roman noticed the Pro boxers sneaking looks at him as he drank water, but was used to people gawking at him. And besides, he was six foot eight inches tall and over two hundred-seventy pounds. Years of work for Alaska Glacier Seafood-loading halibut, some weighing over two hundred pounds, into freezer vans and various construction jobs across Alaska and the Pacific Northwest, mostly as a laborer, had developed Roman into a fine specimen of a working man's man.

The Professional boxers tried to show off themselves a bit, as they punched the heavy bag, lifted weights, and showed their prowess with the speed bag. A couple of them, though including the training camp manager, couldn't seem to concentrate on their work and kept looking over at the big man from Alaska, with his shirt off and his working muscles glistening with sweat- and rippling as he punched holes in the ground with the post hole digger and then lifted the big plants up before lowering them gently into the ground. The clincher though, came when the Japanese gardener needed to go for a hydraulic jack to lift the big Ford tractor front end and put on a freshly-repaired tire and wheel.

"Wait right here," he said before adding, "I'm going to go get a jack so we can change the wheel."

Roman said, "Wait; I'll lift it, you put on the new wheel," as he locked his hands around the axle, straightened his back and proceeded to lift the left front wheel of the tractor off the ground with his massive frame.

Eyes bulged and heads shook as they, the now staring boxers, watched in disbelief at what Roman was capable of lifting.

At 4:30 after his supervisor had gone home, Roman wandered over for a closer look at the Professionals still working hard at their craft. The speed bag crashed away in a familiar rhythm as Frank L. Jackson, the owner of the training camp, hit the bag for an eternity with his fists.

"Speed, timing, and finesse are what a great fighter needs," Roman remembered his Grandfathers' friend from England had told him when he was a teenager in Poland. All through high school, retired boxing trainer Albert Day had patiently coached Roman on the 'Gentlemanly Art of Boxing,' as he called it. The lessons served Roman well in after school boxing bouts, and he later applied them once or twice while serving in the Polish army.

"Hey you," the fight camp manager called to Roman. "Do you want to make some quick cash for half-an-hours work?"

"Yeah sure," came the interested reply.

"OK here's the deal, we need a new sparring partner for our boys, you put on these here gloves, climb in the ring, remain standing for thirty minutes, and I'll pay you thirty bucks cash. Have we got a deal?"

Roman nodded his head in agreement.

Luis Raul Guzman, two hundred-eighteen pounds of finely tuned boxing muscle, was standing ringside and quickly answered the managers call to perform a twenty minute workout and give 'our new volunteer' a lesson on what a Pro can do.

Guzman advanced, the volunteer stepped backward cautiously. Roman gathered his wits and began remembering back to the lessons from Albert Day '…Focus on what you are doing, size-up your opponent carefully, keep your guard up & make him miss when you can. When you have figured his strength and style; begin peppering him with jabs, adding in a few stingers now-and-then to assume control…'

The right-hand jabs Roman began throwing were all accomplishing their intended purpose when suddenly he applied a bit too much 'sting' on one of them, and connected right on the button of Guzman's jawbone. The professionals' eyes glazed over, his knees buckled and down he went...

Ring assistants quickly helped Guzman out of the ring before the Manager gave the nod to Angel Rodriguez, another of the camps up-and-coming heavyweights. Roman was getting warmed up now and didn't back-up as much. But Angel wasn't in the ring more than a couple of minutes before he failed to live up to his first name and punched the Polish 'volunteer' four inches below the belt. Roman answered with four quick rights in succession; all of them found their mark on "Angel's" face with the last by far doing the most damage and leaving the pro wobbling before falling face first onto the mat.

The big man still standing in the ring now had everybody's attention, but one person who was focused on him more than the others, Frank L. Jackson the ex-heavyweight champ halted his speed bag work when he saw the second of his favorite heavyweights drop. He quickly stepped over to the ring, climbed in and told his manager, "Lace up my gloves; I'll finish his thirty dollar lesson!"

I'll give you two hundred dollars if you can knock me down!" Jackson growled at Roman Lefthanded Losinski, as he began stalking him around the ring. The seasoned pro really knew his stuff and was soon backing Roman up, jabbing and landing hard right-hand body shots and some well-placed combinations. Two to the body, one to the head: And then again two to the body, followed by one to the head. The next time Jackson began that combination, he got the first two shots off to Roman's rib cage, just as the big Pole landed two stinging right-hand jabs of his own, square in Jackson's face, before instantaneously following them with a crashing left-hook to the temple sending Jackson into unconsciousness and leaving him flat out on the mat....

"What about my money?" Roman said, as the people at ringside began fanning towels at the unconscious ex-champ Jackson, and passing smelling salts under his nose.

"I've got your money over here," said a voice just a few feet away from the ring. Roman climbed out of the ring and walked over to a man who was wearing a blue night watchman's cap and pulling money out of a wallet.

"Two hundred-thirty dollars cash," said the man. "Is that right?"

Roman nodded yes.

"And will you step over to my car so we can fill out some paperwork?" The little man asked. He reminded Roman of his grandfather's friend Albert Day in a strange sort of way.

This gave Roman a good feeling and he instantly began to like the man in the little blue hat.

"I'm Doc Johnny DeAngelo. I just saw you put away two professionally trained boxers and knock out cold the former heavyweight champion of the world. I'll give you two thousand dollars-a-week if you let me train you, represent you in contract negotiations, and get you some top fights over the next three years. Do we have a deal?"

Roman nodded yes and he began to like his 'new' boxing coach more and more and the two of them drove off down the lane leaving Roman's eight dollar-an-hour job, and a ring full of confusion behind them....

TWO

It's nothing just a boxer's break

"How old are you Roman?" asked Doc Johnny DeAngelo, as they turned onto the desert highway heading west and into a beautiful sunset.

"I'm thirty seven," Roman replied.

"Hmmm... from now on, anybody asks, you're thirty one... OK?"

"OK."

"Is this going to be a problem...?" Roman said, as he lifted his left hand toward Doc.

"Let me see that hand," Doc said as he tried to look over and keep the car on the road. "Ahhh... it's nothing just a boxer's break maybe. Open the lid on that ice chest by your feet and shove your hand into the ice water. We can stop at the next hospital for an x-ray and get a cast put on if we need it. No sweat, in six to eight weeks, it will be as good as new."

Doc knew if he stayed on highway 89, they could be at the

hospital in Prescott, Arizona in just under an hour. He hoped they would have a good doctor working the Emergency Room night shift. Their luck held out.

After filing out a clipboard of forms and Doc Johnny DeAngelo offering to pay cash or Visa, the reception nurse led them into a nearby examination room. In walked a beautiful female doctor.

"Hello I'm Doctor Jennifer Casey. How did you do this? Let me see your hand. Can you move your fingers?"

"Boxing... it hurts to move 'em. I've had my hand in ice for the last hour," Roman said, thinking that her touch and caring attitude was making the hand feel better already.

"I want our x-ray tech to get a picture of that, so we can know if there is anything broken," she said with one eyebrow raised and the hint of a smile, as she walked out the door.

A male x-ray tech came in and asked Roman to step down the hall so they could take a couple of pictures of his hand. With shots taken from various angles the tech was done, and he told Roman, "You can return to the examination room and the doctor will be right with you."

"Well by the looks of your x-ray, you have a break in two bones of your left hand, right behind your index and middle fingers," Doctor Casey said. "I recommend a cast of your entire hand and wrist and 'no boxing' for at least six to eight weeks..." she said, smiling as she added, "Does that sound OK to you?"

"OK," Roman said, nodding in agreement and a bit taken by her good looks and gentle manner.

"Well let's get that cast on you then. Do you have a color preference?" she asked, as she showed him a chart with various colors of the latest cast materials.

"This blue one," he said.

After she had finished wrapping his hand in the gauze bandage and applying the quick-dry blue cast material, she added, "I'll give you a prescription for pain medication, take it only if you need it."

"Thank you for seeing me Doctor Casey," Roman said.

She smiled, and replied, "You are welcome Roman," and then walked off toward the nurse's station with his paperwork. They paid their bill, picked up his medication, (in-case he needed it), and were back on the road in under three hours. Roman nodded off to sleep and was soon dreaming of happy times....

THREE

Running in sand

When Roman woke up they had crossed into California on Highway 10, and were just turning onto Highway 111 heading south.

"Where are we going anyway?" Roman asked.

"To the Salton Sea, I've got a little boxer training camp there in the desert south of Palm Springs. We can train there, get in some relaxation, nobody will bother us and it will give your hand some time to heal."

"Sounds good to me," Roman thought out loud, as the two continued down the long straight highway. Forty-five minutes later they turned off the road, traveled a few feet down a sandy driveway, and stopped to unlock a steel cable that stretched across the driveway.

The camp, "El Shacko" as Doc referred to it, was exactly twelve miles past the North Shore Yacht Club, (a bogus 'dream investment' pitched and sold to several of Hollywood's movie star elite crowd).

Doc's property consisted of a collection of old trailers and a couple of ramshackle buildings, his 'experimental' small sailing fleet, some exercise equipment, and a makeshift boxing ring.

"It's a great place to relax, and a light wind that is perfect for sailing comes up almost every afternoon," Doc said almost apologetically, and then continued, "I love this place. For you however, it's going to be one the places we use to get you in the best shape of your entire life. There is plenty of fresh air and sunshine, and the dry sand-lined stream beds make great running trails for you to get your aerobic exercise during long, slow distance runs. And just moving across the sand will help keep you limber and relaxed, and is reported to be an aid in the healing process of all the muscles, joints, and ligaments in the human body."

"An old Greek remedy," he added.

"Sounds perfect Doc," Roman said, as he looked across the beach noticing two small sailboats tied to a post-near, but not in the water. "I know how to sail a boat too," he said.

"Hmmm... really, well as you well noticed we happen to have two identical 12 foot Racing Beetle Cat Sailboats. I see a new sailing regatta shaping up already," Doc said, adding, "To be fair though, we are going to have to trim down your weight a little bit. What do you weigh now, about two hundred and seventy-five pounds?"

"Two hundred seventy-four, the last time I weighed myself," Roman answered, amazed at the accuracy of Doc's guess.

"We want you down around two hundred and forty for a perfect fighting weight by this time next year. Besides, it will make your reflexes even quicker and it will give you a better chance in our sailboat races," Doc said, as he smiled. "Well it's late and I'm tuckered out. Let me show you to your Penthouse Apartment."

Doc showed Roman to his new living space, an old silver trailer that was actually quite nice inside. "Make yourself at-home. There are clean towels and some workout clothes in the dresser; and the shower and bathroom are in the shack next to the boxing ring. I'm going to turn-in for the night, tomorrow is a new day, and we can get an early start then. Good night Roman."

"Good night Doc, and thanks for the chance," Roman added mostly to thin air, since Doc had already trudged off across the crusty sand toward his trailer.

Doc's trailer, and the attached scrap plywood patio was what he referred to as "El Shacko," it also served as the camp gathering spot, and kitchen and dining area.

The next morning Roman looked out the dusty window and saw doc scratching around the outside of his trailer gathering up the mast and sail rigging to one of his sailboats.

"Did you sleep well?" Doc asked, as Roman walked up to observe the sailing master.

"Like a rock."

"I've got fresh coffee brewed up just inside the door of El Shacko, help yourself," Doc said. "The wind is just right for an early morning sail. Walk around a bit, check the place out -and get the lay of the land. There is a little store just up the beach about a half-a-mile to the north of us at Bob's Playa Riviera. I'll be back soon," he said as he carried the mast and sail down to the waters edge and finished preparing the little sailboat -and then launched her off the beach, and into a light wind.

The morning desert air was clean and hardy, and yet had a vigorous salty smell to it. The Salton Sea, a 30 mile long inland salt lake, is 254 feet below sea level, and has a salt content close to 37 parts per million. That makes it one of the highest salt-concentrations of any body of water on earth, and is more than most fish can take, but one fish that survives, the corbina, is a favorite of the local fishermen. And flocks of seagulls seem to enjoy the taste, as they dine on the multitude of expired fish that dot the shoreline.

Roman's hand was throbbing and bothering him a bit, but it soon slipped his mind when he found interesting things to look at, as he walked the shoreline heading in the opposite direction from Bob's Playa Riviera, and away from any buildings. It began to remind him of quiet areas just north of Fairbanks, Alaska, where the buildings and people become sparse and then finally non-existent.

He didn't always like to walk alone... he thought, remembering back to some of the happiest times of his life when he and Antoinette walked hand-in-hand on the trails, and through the woods surrounding their mountain property. But she was gone now... and he must go alone, knowing that someday they would meet again.

And so he walked on alone, noticing how the gentle onshore wind produced small waves that lapped the shoreline. Waves that carried sticks, as well as odd bits of Styrofoam from discarded coolers and cups, along with the occasional dead fish and other bits of anything that floated, and left them at the high and low water marks, and mixed them with the sand and clay that formed the beach in its gentle slope toward higher ground. Every so often he came upon the end of one of the sand-lined steam beds that Doc spoke of. He could see them, wide and open at the waters edge, and then winding their way up, toward the hills to the east of him and his temporary home on the shore of the Salton Sea at Doc's El Shacko Resort and Boxer Training Camp.

FOUR

Now we have some help...

When Roman returned from his shoreline expedition, Doc had completed his morning sailboat voyage and was busy cooking lunch.

"I sailed over to Bob's Playa Riviera Store and picked us up some supplies for lunch, dinner, and breakfast tomorrow; and made some phone calls. Now we have some help coming and you will only have to put up with my cooking for a couple more days. I called two business partners and they are on their way to help us get you ready."

"Who are they" Roman asked.

"They are both retired professional boxers, who now offer their services to train the next generation. They are the best in the business. One is the best cook I know and will be our camp cook and a sparring partner for you. He fought as a middleweight, is as quick as lightning and hits like the thunder of a heavyweight. That's Gibby Goodman. The other one is Sebastian 'Serby' Mandino. He fought lightweight, and was known as 'The

Intelligent Boxer with Fists of Steel' who had a body punch that produced knock-outs. And most of his opponents learned to respect him as someone who had knock-out power in either hand. Like I said they are the best in the business and we are lucky to have them on our team."

Roman smiled. "Thanks Doc," he said. "Thanks for everything."

"I hope you can ride a bicycle because Sebastian and Gibby are bringing one for you."

"I can ride," Roman said. "In Poland when I was 14, I won the Junior National Sprint Cycling Championship."

"Oh that's how you grew those tree trunks you call legs, and barrel-like chest."

Roman smiled again.

"Well since you raced bikes you probably know of, or have read about Eddy Merckx, right?"

"He was before my time," Roman said, "But I read about him, and I know he won the 3,000 mile long Tour De France Bike Race five-times, set the hour record for speed and distance, raced in the Six Day Trials Races on the track, and did Cyclo-Cross racing in the winter-mud just to keep in shape during the off season. I read that he used to beat his competitors so badly that they called him, "The Cannibal."

"That's the guy! Anyway the bike they are picking up for you is a road bike, a real Tour De France Road Racing Bike. It was made in Belgium by a man named Ferdi Kessels, who used to build racing bicycle frames from scratch and he was the one who assembled the actual racing bikes used by Eddie Merckx. And a close friend of mine, Roger McAlister, owns the Cycling Center in

Santa Cruz and he just happened to have a couple of complete race bikes built by Kessels sitting on the shelf. One of them was a twelve-speed Main D'Or Road Bike fitted with the finest Italian racing components, and we think it should be just about the right size for you."

"How did you know my size?" Roman asked.

"I was a tailor when I was younger and still have a pretty good eye for measurement."

"Roman, like I said, Gibby and Sebastian will be here in a couple of days with some more boxing equipment, and they are bringing that bike for you. Consider it a gift, from me to you. And just so you know, Gibby and Sebastian each have their own areas of expertise. Gibby, besides being our resident athletic diet expert and camp cook, will also be your coach for calisthenics, strength training and most of your boxing ring work-outs. And Sebastian will coach you for your aerobic training by cycling and running. He is in his fifty's and has run the Boston Marathon twelve times and has finished in under three hours every time, and he loves competing in bicycle races that are over a hundred miles long. He has a degree in psychology with emphasis in Sports Psychology and Motivation. He will be our 'battle plan psychologist' and will help you understand each of your opponents and to understand yourself better...."

"Wow, sounds great Doc."

"If you want to you can begin your aerobic conditioning before they get here. Here's a watch, it's a scuba diver style with a movable bezel so you can see exactly how many minutes you have been running. It will impress the heck out of Sebastian. He loves these watches for keeping track of athletic improvement. Try running the stream beds, they lead all the way up to bat caves in the hills over there to the east of us. Just take it easy the first few days. Maybe start off with about sixteen minutes of non-stop running, and then add a couple of minutes each day. Remember, run some, then walk a bit, and then run some more if you feel comfortable."

"I think I'll go for a run now and check out those bat caves Doc."

"All right Roman, remember just take it easy running, and you can stop running anytime, but remember to keep moving by walking."

With that Roman took off heading east in a gentle jog, hooking up with a stream bed to run on the ripples of crusty sand, and to look for the bat caves. Each day for the next three days while Doc sailed, Roman ran, as he began the search for the best fitness of his life. As per Doc's recommendation he ran for only sixteen minutes on the first day, and walked the rest. The second day he added three minutes, the time it takes between bells for a single round of boxing. And then by the third day he added another three minutes and was up to twenty-two minutes of non-stop running, before walking at a brisk pace for the rest of the journey.

Doc's cooking wasn't the worst Roman had ever tasted, but when a 1963 dark blue Buick Wild Cat with a 430 cubic inch motor, came rumbling down the sand driveway, and two serious looking men got out and began unloading bicycles and duffle bags of fight gear, Roman guessed the food would be getting better, and real work-outs were about to begin....

FIVE

We got a winner this time…

"Hey Doc what's shakin?" Gibby asked, in the gruff voice Doc remembered.

"Good to see you Gibby. Thanks for coming."

"We picked up the bike you asked for and brought ours too, just like you asked Doc," Sebastian said, as he finished lifting a fancy silver racing bike off the rack on the back of the car.

"Pleased to meet you Roman," Sebastian said, as he offered his hand for a shake.

"Likewise," Gibby added as he stepped over to offer Roman his hand as well.

Roman smiled his big grin, as he shook their hands and simply said, "Same, same, thanks guys."

"Roman did you really knock out Frank L. Jackson?" Sebastian asked him.

"I got lucky with the left," Roman replied.

"He wasn't just lucky with the left, Doc said, "I saw it, and like I told you on the phone; he put away two of Frank's best boys right before that, you should have been there... Frank is probably still wondering what hit him."

"Let's go find Doc's bat caves Roman," Sebastian said. "Let me just get my jogging shoes on," he added.

"Sounds good, I have been out there a couple of times already, and Doc gave me this watch to keep track of my training times," Roman said as he smiled, showing off his new watch.

"How many minutes of continuous running are you up to now?"

"I started with sixteen and added three minutes each time I ran, and I just ran for twenty-two minutes earlier this morning."

"Perfect." Sebastian said.

In ten minutes the two were heading off back up the sandy road and heading east toward the hills.

"I like to run an easy pace where we can talk as we run, OK Roman?"

"Sounds good to me Sebastian."

"You can call me Serby."

"OK Serby, and can I ask you something about Doc?"

"Sure go ahead."

"Is he good for his money? I mean, he offered me a lot of money each week to train and fight in the ring professionally."

"Roman there are three things you can count on in this world: Death, Taxes, and Doc's money. He's always kept his word with me and everyone else will tell you the same thing. Doc pays what he says he will, and he usually adds in a big bonus. In your case, since you're the fighter, your bonus will probably be a percentage of the profits after expenses. You just win the fights he sets up for you and you'll make tons of money."

Roman nodded and smiled. Serby had confirmed the gut feeling Roman had about Doc since they had first met.

"And in case you're interested Doc is very wealthy. He made most of his money from selling off a chain of clothing stores that he started from scratch as a tailor, and then bought a young Thoroughbred race horse, 'Oscar the Grouch,' that became very successful and won big on the race track. Doc doesn't need to work anymore he just does this fight game for something to do. I have known Doc a long time and he just seems to have the 'Midas Touch' when it comes to picking winners. And it appears he must have seen the elements of what it takes to be a winner in you."

"Tell me Roman, what is it that makes you want to be a professional boxer?"

"My grandfather's best friend was a retired boxing coach who was living next door to us in Poland, and he and my grandfather taught me lots of things when I was growing-up. I remember us going to see a movie with the American actor Marlon Brando playing a fighter, and his coach ended a close fight by throwing a towel into the ring, and Marlon's character had this line, and I never forgot it: It goes something like, "What did you do that for Charlie? I could have taken that guy; I could have been a Contender!"

"Well that line has stuck in my head all my life and I always thought maybe I had it in me that 'I could be a Contender.' You are only the second person in my life I have told that to. Please keep my dream a secret."

"OK Roman."

"Thanks Serby."

The two men jogged on closer to the hills. Just before they reached the sand dunes at the base of the crusty sand cliffs, they both stopped jogging and began walking.

"Roman can you tell me who the other person is that you told your dream to?"

Roman looked at him, and said, "Yes I can tell you," and then he walked over and sat on a crusty ledge of the dry stream bed they had been jogging in. Serby stopped and sat down too, his attention focused and patient.

"Her name was Antoinette. We had been married a little more than a year when she and our baby both died in during childbirth. Something about the anesthesia going wrong and the doctors couldn't save either of them. I lost 'em both in the same night," he told Serby through tear filled eyes. Then he added, "Antoinette knew about me watching that movie and thinking maybe 'I could be a Contender,' but we were busy making a life for ourselves in Alaska. I made good money as a laborer and we had our own log house in the mountains and everything and we were very, very happy. Then the next thing, we were at the hospital, and like I said, something went wrong and our baby had died during birth, and I was fast losing Antoinette too. I was holding her hand and the last thing she said was, 'Roman chase that dream... I'll be watching you, and I love you,' and then she just died...."

"I need to be by myself for a while Serby, I think I'll stay out here by the bat caves and think. Is that OK with you?"

"Sure, sure Roman, I'll walk on ahead back to El Shacko. Gibby will probably have dinner ready about six o'clock, if you want some, come back anytime you like, and we'll see you when you get back."

When Serby got back to El Shacko, Doc was out sailing and Gibby was just adding the finishing touches to a pot of chili he had whipped-up for dinner.

"So what do you think about Roman?" Gibby asked, as Serby walked-up, smiling and looking into the chili pot Gibby was stirring.

"I think Doc's right. We got a winner this time. He definitely has the desire to reach the top. We'll both know a lot more when we see him in the ring, and you begin feeling his punches when he hits you."

"I am not sure I want him to hit me at all if he swings like he did at Frank's camp in Sedona," Gibby replied with a smile.

"I know what you mean, he is as big as a tank and with him hitting like Doc says, this could get very interesting. We will have to find some extra padding for your rib protector and boxing helmet," Serby said jokingly.

"I'm going to gather-up some driftwood for tonight's bonfire. I'm betting Doc's got a plan all worked out, and will want to share it with us tonight around the fire," Serby said.

The sun was just setting in the hills to the west, as Doc beached the yellow Beetle Cat sailboat. Smiling like a cat with a mouse, he walked up the beach towards the burning bonfire and joined Serby and Gibby. Just as he did, Roman appeared in the distance-walking down the driveway.

When all four of them were sitting around the fire, Gibby

made the announcement, "If you're hungry there's chili on the stove and fresh bread on the counter, help yourselves guys."

Gibby hardly had the sentence out, before Serby was up and heading towards El Shacko. He wanted to be the first one in-line at the chili pot. He was no fool and was used to eating the delicious food that Gibby was famous for whipping up.

As the four of them mopped-up their third helping of chili, Doc said, "I have got this all planned out."

"I phoned Bob Abrams and told him we are preparing a heavyweight fighter for a run at the top, he is a boxing promoter and an old friend of mine, and we agreed on a list of ten journeymen boxers that should test your drive and your ability to grow as a professional fighter. Get through that group first and we should be able to book you to fight one of the top Contenders. I am figuring we can set up the first fight for ten to twelve weeks from now and that will give plenty of time for your hand to be fully healed. Does that sound agreeable to everybody?"

They all nodded in agreement.

"Looks like as soon as he is ready it's full-speed-ahead training mode," Gibby said

"By the way he runs, hc is in pretty good condition now, and with the next ten weeks of run, cycle, box routine wc should be ready on time," Serby said, as Roman smiled.

"All right gentlemen, let the fun begin. You two know the routine, everyday 6-9 a.m. roadwork, either cycling, or a long slow distance run, you decide which, 9:30 breakfast, 10-12 calisthenics and ring work-out; noon lunch, and then more roadwork with some more time in the ring before dinner at 6:30. After dinner we can discuss the day around the campfire. Oh- and I've got another training camp lined up in the mountains near Big Bear for the last four weeks before each fight, for workouts in the hills," Doc said, smiling again like a cat.

Doc's plan was working out fine, and each morning like clockwork, Roman, Serby and Gibby would head out on the bikes for a ride south on Highway 111 going farther and farther and faster and faster each time, or sometimes it would just be Serby and Roman on a run up the beach, or out to the bat caves, or sometimes Roman would run by himself. The others began giving knowing looks to each other, as they each noticed in Roman, the burning desire that a champion needs to succeed.

During each training session in the ring, Roman became more and more polished as he listened well to their expert guidance and learned from the wise boxers who were sharing what they knew, with the man they each hoped would get a chance to become the next heavyweight champion of the world.

One of Gibby's favorite power-punch strengthening exercises was to carry a large round rock and to toss it like a shot put, and then to run ahead and pick it up and toss it again, and again running up and down the dry river beds that made their way to the hills in the east. Roman began putting in extra training time sometimes even late on star-lit nights, tossing and chasing the heavy round rock Gibby had picked-out for him. The strength in his right side became noticeably more powerful as he tossed the rock, ran ahead, picked it up and tossed it again, repeating the procedure over and over.

After six weeks and a trip to the hospital in Indio to check out a new x-ray of Roman's left hand, it was decided to take his cast off, and begin exercises to strengthen the muscles of his left arm and hand.

Doc Johnny DeAngelo came up with a newspaper after each days sailing voyage to Bob's Playa Riviera, and had Roman begin to strengthen his left hand by starting in one corner of just the front page, and wrinkle it up in as tight of a ball as he could, using just one hand, and then work his way through the whole paper, page by page, wrinkling each sheet in a small ball and tossing it aside. Serby loved the crunched-up newspapers as a source of camp fire starter and Roman really liked the workout and the feeling of strength coming back into his formerly powerful left-hand and wrist.

After a few days, he was chasing his 'shot put' rock tossed from his left arm as well as his right.

Days blended into weeks and finally it was time to make the move to the Big Bear Mountain Training Camp. This move really pleased Serby and Gibby who both knew the importance of hill climbing psychologically as well as physically.

The mountain camp had a large barn shaped building with a polished wooden floor and was set up as an indoor boxing gym complete with a boxing ring, heavy bag, a speed bag, deluxe showers and a tiled steam room.

The living accommodation was a big, two-story, four-bedroom, log cabin that had; a large rock fireplace on the first floor in the living room, a big dining room a well-equipped kitchen, and four comfortable bedrooms upstairs.

After getting settled in at their new training camp, Doc took them into town on a shopping expedition. He had a mini-vacation in mind for them, and had them each pick out a frame-backpack, and assorted camping gear at a backpacker specialty store.

"Tomorrow I want you guys to take a few days off from the ring. Go for a backpacking trip and hike over the summit of Mt.

San Gorgonio, it's 11,502 feet tall and I can drop you guys off at the start of the trail by Angels Camp, and you guys can take off from there. There is good trout fishing at Dollar Lake. From there it's only an eight mile hike to the summit. And when you get to the top just go down the other side you'll figure out which camp sites to stop at. Call me when you get back to civilization from the phone at Big Falls General Store; and I'll come pick you up and drive you back here."

After breakfast the next day Doc dropped them off at the trail head, and Gibby, Serby and Roman, hiked off into the distance, up "Poop-out Hill," and through the woods to Dollar Lake. They set up camp, and just like Doc said, the trout fishing was good. Roman caught three Rainbow trout by six p.m. and Gibby and Serby each caught two. Gibby cooked them for dinner over the camp fire, and even baked a delicious apple pie for desert in a small reflector oven he had brought along for just such a treat!

Doc sure knew how to pick the people around him, Roman thought. With Gibby doing the cooking the three of them were eating like Kings. Roman began to wonder how Doc was doing back at the mountain cabin, scratching around eating his own cooking. Roman mentioned this to Gibby and Serby when he said, "I bet Doc isn't eating this good?"

The three of them laughed heartily, and then each in turn, reached for a second helping of hot apple pie and relaxed around the warmth of the campfire.

The fire glowed, popped and sparkled in shades of blue, green, red, yellow and orange as they stared into it mesmerized, yet listening to each other tell stories from their past. Roman liked hearing Gibby and Serby tell about tough fights in the ring, especially those that were close battles that they eventually won in the end; either by knock-out, or the other fighter's refusal to answer the bell, or even a hard fought decision.

"Serby, how did you get the nick-name 'The Intelligent Boxer with Fists of Steel'? Roman asked him.

"One of the reporters for Boxing Ring Magazine knew I had graduated from college; and he made up the nickname after he saw me throw a solid right-hand punch to the mid-section of Johnny Curly, and knock him out in the seventh round of our first slug fest. Johnny and I had two more fights after that. And outside the ring, we actually became pretty good friends. But I could see it in his eyes that I had earned his respect."

"How did you learn to hit hard enough with a body punch to produce knock-outs?" Roman asked him.

Serby smiled and replied, "I was training with an old boxer and he hit me so hard in the solar plexus once, that I was knocked out instantly, and was hurting and sick for days. I made up my mind right there and then, that I was going to learn to hit with power like that, so that fighters remembered me. I wanted the people I fought to remember the punches from my fists."

"I began by visualizing that my right arm and fist were a three inch round bar of steel. And then I would see myself in fights, waiting patiently for an opening in my opponents' mid-section for my right, and then pick my spot, either aiming at the bottom rib on the left side, or right in the pit of the stomach. I would see that fist punching through clear-through to his backbone. Over and over I saw the opening and saw myself throwing the punch."

"And that was it! I began using it in fights more and more. The more I used it, the more opponents respected my punches. Simple really," Serby said with a smile.

SIX

To the summit

The stories Gibby and Serby told of the tough fights they had during their careers in the ring, and the skills and the strategy's they used to become winners were still on Roman's mind as he drifted off to sleep.

The next morning Roman woke to the aroma of freshly cooked flap-jack pancakes that Gibby had whipped up for breakfast.

"Fresh pancakes, come and get 'em," Gibby shouted. Cooked to a perfect golden brown, and sprinkled with blueberries that Gibby had packed for the trip, they were delicious.

As he ate---Roman's mind drifted back to the days in his past and of the pancakes Antoinette had cooked for him after collecting wild blueberries that grew on the hillsides of their mountain property....

-He missed her-yet at times like this, comfortably felt her presence all around him-

"We can make it to High Creek Campground by this afternoon if we leave after breakfast," Serby figured out-loud as he looked over the trail map, and brought Roman back from his daydream to the present- and to thoughts of the journey ahead of him.

The hike to High Creek Campground meandered across meadows, and over ridges that were covered in tall Ponderosa Pine trees. The canyon walls grew steeper as the hikers gained altitude, and then finally after one last bend in the trail, the campground came into view. There it was, nestled into a grassy meadow with a clear blue stream running through it. This would be a comfortable place to relax and get a good nights-rest before the climb to the summit.

Before Gibby had figured out what to prepare for dinner, Roman and Serby had leaned their packs against a tree, taken out their fishing poles, and had tossed baited hooks in the cold water of the fast running stream. Within minutes Roman and Serby had each caught three Rainbow trout.

"OK you two that settles it: trout for dinner and there will be hot blueberry pie for desert," Gibby said.

That night after dinner Roman asked Gibby where he learned to cook so-good.

Gibby stared into the campfire for a moment before he answered. "When I was a kid I spent most of my childhood being tossed around from one foster home to another, until this old black man who had been a professional boxer took me in and adopted me. He had retired from boxing and when I met him he worked as a breakfast cook at a local coffee shop. He figured I needed to learn how to cook meals for myself, so he taught me to cook like a professional. He also taught me how to box since I kept getting beat-up by the neighborhood bullies. He taught me the Detroit Gladiator-style of boxing, you know chin tucked in, and always covered up, and constantly advancing and pushing the pace of the fight, and how to throw the devastating overhand straight right that became my trademark knock-out punch," Gibby said with a smile in his eyes.

The stars were twinkling bright that night and the snap crackle-pop of the campfire became the only sounds heard as the three men became silent and stared into the fire, thinking of the future that lay ahead of them.

Roman was the first to turn-in and he was fast asleep and dreaming of happy times, while the other two men stayed awake looking into the fire, sipping coffee, and sharing their plans and ideas about training methods and schedules for the future.

At breakfast the next morning Gibby served-up some rib-sticking oatmeal and brewed up a pot of good coffee. Excitement began to stir as they did the morning dishes, and started packing up to leave the camp and head for the summit. Serby and Gibby kidded each other about who would be the first one to make it to the top. Roman confidently kidded both of them that they would find him comfortably resting at the top when they got there. So the race was on.

Although Roman was the slowest to finish packing and the last one to leave camp, he soon caught up with and passed the other two, and then gradually increased the distance between them, as he headed up the steep switchback trail. As he got closer to the summit and out of their sight he celebrated by picking up a large round rock and began tossing it ahead of him, retrieving it and doing it again and again and again, just as Gibby had taught him. What a great exercise he thought; then he began reflecting on how these two men and Doc were fast becoming some of his best friends he had on earth, and how they were teaching him exactly what he needed to learn and do to reach his goals.

As he climbed higher and higher the trees became fewer and fewer until he realized he was finally above tree line. Now the trail switched back and forth between large granite boulders, and up and over ridge after ridge, each time revealing yet another higher peak ahead to climb to. Faster and faster he went as he tried to increase his pace, racing for the top, yet gasping for air to fill his lungs and supply the oxygen his muscles needed to continue the journey. Higher and higher he went as the view became more and more spectacular. Each turn in the trail revealed more and more. Finally there it was; a summit survey marker "Mt. San Gorgonio elevation 11,502 feet."

Waist high boulders all around the summit were the tallest things anywhere in sight. It was here, standing on the peak of the tallest mountain for hundreds of miles around that Roman realized the supreme mountain to climb, is the mountain of the best person you can be. The lessons he was learning from his friends and from his own experience were teaching him how to be the best he could be---in a quest to stand on the peak of himself.

He silently began giving thanks for his friends and for the many people that helped him along on his path in life.

-Then a presence encircled him, warming his heart... Antoinette... Here on the summit he could again feel her closeness, her love and her belief in him as a champion. He inwardly knew in his heart he was on the right path and would have all the power he needed to fulfill his goal and become a contender for the heavyweight championship of the world-

He sat down and leaned against a rock, closed his eyes and soon drifted off to sleep dreaming about Antoinette and happy times....

When Gibby and Serby reached the summit there was

Roman resting comfortably with a smile on his face, just as he had predicted to them earlier that morning.

"Alright... wake up sleepy head, you show off," Serby kidded him, as he and Gibby trudged up the last few feet of the trail- and saw Roman peacefully sleeping.

Roman's eyes popped-open, he smiled, and got up to share the panoramic view from the top with them.

After a few minutes rest at the summit the three of them were ready to descend to their next campsite. Serby checked the trail map, and suggested Vivian Creek Campground as their next destination. It would be a long hike to the camp, but it would put them within an easy mornings hike to the mountain community of Big Falls where Doc would meet them for the ride home.

After an hour of hiking downhill, along a dusty switchback trail, they were finally below tree line and a few hours later-just before sunset, Vivian Creek and their final camping spot came into view.

"I can sure feel it in my legs, and I know I'm going to sleep good tonight," Gibby said.

"I've always thought going downhill was tougher than going up," Serby added, as they each dropped their packs at a level campsite within sight of the gurgling creek. Several large boulders formed a natural dam for a small pond. With no one else nearby, the three hikers all seemed to get the same idea and had soon shed their shirts and pants and were diving into the cool blue water.

The next morning Gibby cooked delicious flapjack pancakes for breakfast along with another pot of coffee. As they ate breakfast, the three of them sensed the unspoken bond of friendship that had developed between them during their hike.

While they packed for the trip down the hill they also sensed the end of the journey was nearby.

Two hours of hiking later they had made it down the steep trail, traveled past the giant waterfalls and hiked into the little community of Big Falls. Serby used the phone at the general store to call Doc, while Gibby and Roman challenged each other's skill on a vintage hardwood shuffleboard table. Just over an hour later Doc arrived to pick them up.

"Well, how was your hike gentleman?"

"We had a great time Doc," Roman said, as Gibby and Serby each smiled, and gave the thumbs-up signal to Doc.

SEVEN

Fifty-seven seconds

Once back at their mountain boxing camp the men quickly got back into their training routine.

Looking for and finding all the steepest sections of paved roads became a routine part of their training sessions on the bicycles. The 8,439 foot climb over Onyx Summit became one of Roman's favorites. He attacked the steepest sections of the hill in unrelenting displays of power and aggression. Witnessing Roman's hill climbing performances and sensing his desire, Gibby and Serby let Doc know that they felt he was ready for his fist opponent. That night after dinner, Doc announced that he had made the phone call and had arranged for Roman's first fight to be with a heavyweight brawler by the name of Hugo Bartolo. The fight was to take place in three weeks-time just fifty miles away at the Scribner Auditorium in San Bernardino.

With only three weeks left until fight day, their plan was to continue the physical and mental conditioning. Gibby and Roman worked on improving a technique for Roman being able to switch back and forth between his usual left-hand stance and the right-hand Detroit Gladiator-style that Gibby knew so well and had mastered in the ring.

And Serby taught Roman the power of positive imaging by having him start off every morning by repeating the sentence over and over: Every day in every way I get better and better bit by bit. Every day in every way I get better and better bit by bit....

They began visualizing the upcoming fight in their minds eye and seeing it go the way they wanted it to go. And they would finish each session by seeing the ring announcer hold up Roman's hand at the end of the fight.

Serby did the research on Hugo Bartolo and found out he was known for his vicious left and right hooks, with equally devastating power in either hand, and for pulling dirty tricks in the ring, including questionably low blows anytime he thought the referee was not looking.

Together Serby, Roman and Gibby came up with a fight plan to keep Hugo out-of-range and off-balance with Roman's powerful right-hand jab, and as soon as he saw the opportunity to throw the devastating combination punches they had worked on together.

The weeks flew by and before they knew it, it was time to make the journey off the mountain and down into the city of San Bernardino. The plan was to arrive the day before the fight, to stay at the Holiday Inn; be ready for weigh-in the next afternoon, and be well rested for the fight scheduled for 7:30 p.m. that night.

Hugo Bartolo weighed in at two hundred and forty-eight pounds. He was dark haired and about a head shorter than Roman, but round faced and tough looking with wide shoulders and huge arms.

As he stepped off the scale he looked over at Roman and said, "Ready to kiss the canvas tonight pal?"

"I'm not your pal," Roman replied.

Roman stepped onto the scale and the bar tipped at two hundred and sixty-three pounds.

"Bigger they are the harder they fall," Hugo jeered at Roman as he and his handlers went around the corner and out of the room.

"You OK, Roman?" Serby asked.

"Yeah, I'm OK."

On the ride back to the hotel Roman sensed the tension still in the air and fully knew and understood the importance of this fight.

"He's just the next hill to climb Roman," Serby said, breaking the tension and the silence. Two hours ticked-by and then it was time to head over to the Scribner Auditorium. The men left the hotel with Doc leading the way to the parking lot, and they rode to the arena in silence; each man thinking about the upcoming fight. The sun was still shinning when the four of them went into the building. As they walked along the corridor to the dressing room they could hear the crowd.

Roman changed into his fight gear, and Doc carefully wrapped his hands. Roman used the remaining time to warm-up by shadow boxing in front of the mirror. Finally the door of the dressing room opened, a head popped in and said, "Fight time boys."

Roman donned his robe, and the four of them were out the door and on their way down the aisle to the brightly lit boxing ring.

The auditorium was packed and the crowd cheered as Hugo Bartolo ducked under the ropes and into the ring. They liked the heavyweight battles, and this crowd had seen Hugo demolish opponents before. Roman stepped up onto the ring apron and under the top rope as the crowd continued the applause. As per Roman's instructions Doc had registered him as being from his adopted town in Alaska and this drew a loud applause from the crowd as the ring announcer said into the microphone, "And in this corner, fighting out of Fairbanks, Alaska... Roman Lefthanded Losinski."

The referee called them to the center of the ring and they walked forward looking each other over.

"Hello Loser," Hugo said to him.

"Listen!" the referee said, as he told them the usual ring instructions...

They went back to their corners. Doc checked the laces on Roman's gloves and offered a last minute instruction: "Fight your own fight Roman..." He listened to Doc while stretching out his arms on the ropes, scuffing his feet in the rosin below and flexing his legs. The gong rang, and Roman spun, and walked to the center of the ring. Hugo met him and they touched gloves and started jabbing, circling, slipping and ducking each other's punches as they began sensing the others power and speed. Roman noticed he was quicker with the jab than his opponent and began the process of finding his range. Then suddenly Hugo lunged-in stepping on Roman's right foot-effectively blocking his retreat, while swinging with a powerful right hook to the ribs and a vicious left that had caught Roman unaware as it smashed into his temple....

Fifty-seven seconds into the fight... and Roman was down on one knee, for a second everything went dark. The punches kept coming. Then the ref jumped between them and ordered Hugo to a neutral corner. The mandatory count followed... five, six, seven... and as Roman's eyes began to clear he looked around and saw his corner motioning to him, but he couldn't hear a thing over the roar of the crowd, then he heard a voice, "Get up...get up... get up." Roman stood up on the count of eight and the ref looked into his eyes and stepped out of the way, Hugo swarmed in sensing an easy victory. Roman remembering his training and needing time to clear his head, wrapped his huge arms around Hugo's wildly swinging hooks, and effectively stopped the onslaught. It was like the old days when Roman would stoop down on a construction site in Alaska, lock his arms around a full 55 gallon oil barrel and then stand up with it and put it in the back of a truck. But Hugo got an arm loose and pounded it repeatedly into Roman's side until Roman again effectively wrapped him up. The ref gave him a few more seconds before stepping between them to break them apart. Hugo came in again with hooks swinging from all directions. This time though, he was not standing on Roman's foot, and Roman was able to circle backwards and land several jabs squarely on Hugo's flat nose with his lightning-quick right hand. The round continued. Roman's vision cleared and his legs no longer felt like rubber. Now Hugo was throwing hooks wildly, sensing a missed opportunity and missing with almost every swing. Roman bobbed and weaved, and remained just out of his reach, as he peppered Hugo with jabs and circled away for him. The rest of the round belonged to Roman as he scored more and more points with his jabs and followed them with point scoring combinations. The bell rang. Round one was over.

In the corner, Roman's team went to work massaging his legs and shoulders and telling him he had made an excellent recovery.

"Keep him at bay, keep jabbing with the right," Gibby told him. "You are out-boxing him and beating him to every punch. He is getting frustrated with that. And keep clear of his feet!"

The bell for round two sounded, and the fighters stood up.

Hugo lunged forward as they got to the center of the ring. He again thrust out his foot and swung wildly with the right hook. This time Roman had moved to the side and answered with three quick rights into the side of Hugo's head and followed them with a powerful left, right, left combination before dancing clear and circling out of range. Again Hugo lunged, this time his forward momentum was stopped by a thunderous straight right hand from Roman and capped off with a crushing left hook to the jaw and followed by a right that knocked Hugo over backwards and clear off his feet.

Laying on the canvas, flat on his back, Hugo's eyes opened just as the referee's count went: "Eight... nine... ten." The referee motioned with his hands... fight over. The defeated fighter's corner men jumped into the ring and helped their man up and onto a corner stool.

Seconds later the referee was raising Roman's hand in victory, as he said into the microphone, "Thirty-nine seconds in round two by knock-out, the winner Roman Lefthanded Losinski."

Roman walked over to his opponent's corner, looked into Hugo's still blurry eyes and then said to his manager, "Sorry about knocking your man out; I just can't have anybody stepping on my toes."

Roman returned to his corner, greeting them each with a big smile.

"Let's go out and get some dinner and celebrate a-well-earned victory gentlemen." Doc said, as Serby and Gibby jumped into the ring and began congratulating Roman as they removed his boxing gloves and cut the tape off his hands.

EIGHT

A Champion Gets Up One More Time

"Outstanding work gentlemen," Doc said across the table as the four of them celebrated a result of their hard work and conditioning. "Roman, there is a saying in the fight game that 'A Champion gets up one more-time." And tonight you showed everyone that you have the ability to get back up, and recover quickly from devastating punches, and to earn yourself a victory in a commanding way. Keep up the great work!"

"Thanks Doc and thanks Gibby and thanks Serby, I couldn't have done it without you guys."

The men all smiled and raised their glasses to each other in salute.

"So what's the game plan Doc? We all know you have our next move worked out," Serby said.

"Well..." Doc said, looking at each of them and smiling as he began. "I already spoke to Bob Abrams and we have you lined up to fight again here in seven weeks Roman. We are still working out the details on which fighter you will face. I figure we can head back to the desert and rest up at El Shacko for the first three weeks. And I'm thinking maybe you guys ought to take the next three or four days off from the ring and just run the sand trails and maybe log some extra time in on the bikes while I relax and get in some more sailing. Does that sound agreeable to everyone?"

"Sounds perfect Doc," Serby said, as Gibby and Roman nodded in agreement.

After a sound night's sleep at the hotel and a hot breakfast at the restaurant next door, the four of them set off early for Doc's El Shacko Resort and Boxer Training Camp.

Just after one o'clock in the afternoon they turned down the long sandy driveway leading to El Shacko. It felt good to be back. After a filling lunch, Roman took a leisurely walk south along the beach just as he had done the first day he had spent at Doc's place just three months earlier.

He found himself alone with his thoughts as he walked along the shoreline, silently giving thanks for the opportunities given to him, for his friends, and everyone that had helped him. He turned up the next trail towards the bat caves and broke into a gentle jogging pace as tears of joy, thanks, and happiness began streaming down his face. Releasing long pent-up emotions and gradually increasing his pace, he ran faster and faster in celebration. It seemed like he had been running forever and ever, still he ran on. It became easier and easier to hold his rapid pace as he found himself accelerating around the curves, and across the crusty ripples and up the dry stream-bed trail. His heart pounded away in his chest, pumping blood throughout his body and feeding his muscles, as the large sand dunes and entrance to the bat caves drew rapidly closer.

Later that afternoon, when he got back to El Shacko, Gibby was inside cooking-up dinner, Doc was out sailing, and Serby was busy collecting driftwood and scrap building materials for the nightly bonfire. When Roman went over to help with the firewood, he noticed Serby was separating the collection into two separate piles, one near the campfire site and one consisting mainly of long strips of plywood over by the side of El Shacko.

"Hey check these out," Serby said, as he held up three nice pieces of plywood. "Just perfect for making new signs I want to hang up around the place." Seeing Roman's confused look he added, "I have a bunch of favorite quotes that I like to help me keep my focus, and reach my goals. Like these," he added, as he pulled out a small notebook that was full of sentences all written in capital letters. As Roman began reading over the list he could see why Serby like them so much:

BOXERS ARE ORDINARY PEOPLE WITH EXTRAORDINARY DETERMINATION

WHAT WE HOLD STEADY IN IMAGINATION MUST EVENTUALLY REFLECT IN OUR OUTER WORLD

TO DO IS TO BE

YOU ARE NEVER DEFEATED BY ANYTHING UNTIL YOU ACCEPT THE THOUGHT IN YOUR MIND THAT YOU ARE DEFEATED

TRYING IS SUCCESS

UPON THE ANVIL THE NAIL IS FORMED

HOLD THE MENTAL PICTURES OF WHAT YOU WANT TO HAPPEN

THE REAL SECRET IS TO LEARN TO DREAM DREAMS INTO REALITY

TO BE SUCCESSFUL MEANS TO REALIZE A FAVORABLE TERMINATION OF CONSCIOUSLY PLANNED PROJECTS

YOU ARE THE MASTER AND COMMANDER OF YOUR MENTAL PATTERNS

A MAJOR RULE IS: NEVER BECOME EMOTIONALLY REACTIVE TO ANY UNWANTED EXPERIENCE

THE ONLY WAY OUT OF A PROBLEM IS INTO THE SOLUTION

GENERAL IDEAS FOR SUCCESS:

1. PREPARATION

2. PERSPIRATION

3. FOLLOW THROUGH

"These are great Serby," he said, just as Doc came trudging up the beach carrying the mast and rigging and depositing them along the backside of his trailer.

"I see Serby is sharing some of his secret methods with you eh Roman?" Doc said, nodding in approval as he walked past the two men and plopped into a lawn chair near the edge of the fire.

The quotes were still fresh on Roman's mind as the three of them set out from camp the next morning for some roadwork on the bicycles. The plan for the day was to ride all the way to the hot springs, take a relaxing soak, get some lunch at the restaurant next door, and then ride home. Months of riding together as teammates had allowed them to trust each other and ride in close pace-line formation. After only a few minutes warming up to speed, they were soon whizzing down the highway with each man taking turns at the front for only a minute or two, before pulling slightly to the left to let the others on by; and then pulling in close behind, to benefit from the draft created by the other two. After a few minutes rest at the back, each rider took another pull at the front. Down the road they flew zapping up the miles. While pulling at the front of the pace-line, their heart rates increased upwards of one hundred and sixty beats-per minute, pumping the blood needed and re-supplying their muscles with energy, as they flew down the highway. Each time it became Roman's turn to pull at the front, he shifted onto the larger front sprocket and applied his awesome power, pressing ever harder on the pedals, and accelerating the pace. Burning up the miles they soon found they had covered the thirty-eight mile distance to the hot springs in less than two hours. As the sign came up, the riders looked behind them, slowed up and signaled for the left turn into the driveway.

After a relaxing soak in the hot springs followed by a plate lunch at the El Toro Bravo Mexican Restaurant next door, the three men rolled back to El Shacko at a more relaxed pace.

"What did you guys think of our waitress today?" Serby inquired, as the three of them finally rolled to a stop at El Shacko.

"She was good looking," Gibby offered.

"Her long dark braids reminded me of Antoinette," Roman added.

"You think of Antoinette a lot don't you Roman?" Serby asked.

"Everyday... and in some ways I feel like she is always with me," he replied. "Remember when I fought in San Bernardino and Hugo knocked me down with that hook? Well when I looked up and saw you guys motioning for me to get up, I could see your lips moving, but I couldn't hear anything over the crowd ---then for a second or so I thought I saw her in the seats behind you and I swear I heard a sweet voice saying, "Get up, get up, get up!"

The men all just looked at each other in silence. No one said anything as they leaned their bikes against the wall of El Shacko. Finally Serby spoke up, "Tell us about her. Did you meet her when you were up in Alaska?"

Roman's face broke into a smile as he began, "Yeah, I was doing construction work one winter, and when the job was finished I got laid-off. So I went by our local college and ended-up enrolling in a couple of classes. I signed up for a writing class, and a music appreciation class. The music class was taught by the conductor of the Fairbanks Symphony, and for our textbook he made us buy a full-season pass to the concerts. And we were supposed to pick two of the concerts we attended and write a paper on them. The very first one I went to I saw Antoinette. She played violin and sat in the first chair. I knew right away that if she was not married that I wanted to ask her out. I saw the conductor later and asked him about her. He told me that she was single and not dating anyone. The very next concert I made sure a bouquet of flowers was delivered to her backstage when the concert was over. No note, just the flowers. Each time for the next three concerts I did the same thing. Then the fourth bouquet of roses I delivered myself, told her who I was, and asked her to go out on a date with me. She smiled, and politely refused. I asked her if she minded if I kept sending her roses. She said OK. So I kept it up, and then one time when I had written a little poem for my writing class I included a copy of it with the flowers. Well that must have helped, because after class one day my music teacher hinted that I should ask her out again. So I did- and she said yes! We started going out. She was tall and I think she liked the fact that I was taller than her. And she told me that she liked it when I would scoop her up in my arms and carry her off. Later I found out that her middle name was Rose. Would you guys like to see her picture and a copy of the poem I wrote? I can go get them, I've got them both right inside my trailer."

"Sure, sure" they said, smiling as they each sat down in a chair by the fire ring.

He went into his trailer and came back outside proudly carrying a worn-out photo, and a copy of his favorite poem. He sat down in a chair across from them; as they looked over the photo of the woman he had married, and read the little poem that helped him win her heart.

I'm

A Bee

The Woman is the Flower

Around and Around I

Buzz and Buzz.

Looking for, Just the Right;

Scent Texture, Vibration

Always Looking, Always Looking

For the Tender Loving Flower

Who Willing Gives of Herself

I'm a Bee: The Woman is the Flower

Together We Might Produce, Quite Simply,

The Very Sweetest Honey...

Doc came walking up the beach after his sailing voyage and sat down as Roman continued sharing bits of his life.

Seeing Doc on the edge of his chair, the others could tell he was eager to share something with them. Roman finally said to him, "What's the news Doc? Have you decided who my next opponent is going to be?"

"Maybe" he answered. "I wanted to check it out with you first. There is a guy who picked your name off a list and says he knows you and wants to fight you. His name is Andre' Golkin. He is the reigning European Heavyweight Champion and he is on exhibition tour of the U.S. In seven weeks he will be at the Scribner Auditorium, and he wants you as his opponent."

"I know him," Roman began. "He is from Poland and same size as me, and we grew up in the same tough neighborhood. We have fought before. We fought as kids, then as teenagers, and again when I was in the army I fought him after he had just come home from the Olympic Games. He had defeated the American, the Russian, and even the big Cuban boxer and had come home with a Gold Medal. In our demonstration bout, in-front of my military buddies, he beat me by a decision on points; but he has never been able to knock me down."

"Are you willing to step into the ring with him again?" Doc asked.

Roman gathered his thoughts.

Gibby said, "Roman was good when we started and has

steadily improved his sense of timing, speed and accuracy. And his punching power is one of the best I have ever seen. I think he is ready."

"I want to collect some background tapes on Golkin, so we can be prepared, but I think Roman is unstoppable," Serby added.

Roman smiled seeing the confidence his close friends and professional trainers had in him, and feeling in his gut; his own readiness, he said, "Same, same. Let's fight! This time we even the score!"

"Then it's settled," Doc said. "I'll make the arrangements and set it up for seven weeks from today."

Later that night, Roman went for a walk down the beach just to think about the future, and ended up doing another run to the bat caves along the crusty sand trails, and then once there, up and down the long sloping sand dunes that faced the entrances to the caves. Over and over, up and down the sand dunes he ran, sweat pouring off him as he churned up every step in deep-soft-sand, as a powerful locomotive chugs up a steep hill with its awesome display of reserve power on tap, as if any hill would dare to be steep enough not to be beatable. Then after what seemed like twenty rounds of defeat to the resistance of the sand hill, he found a large rock to toss alternating and mixing it up, tossing it first from his right arm, and then from his left as he ran all the way back from the hills to the boxing camp at El Shacko. It felt good to workout tossing the rock as he jogged along in the evening desert air, cooling down and setting in memory every step he took, and every rock toss as taking one step and one punch closer to victory.

For the next three weeks the men trained harder than they ever had before. Doc and Serby located tapes of Golkin's last three fights and each evening after dinner the men analyzed his strength and punching style. Gibby changed his form to an upright European boxer style, and practiced the moves over and over, as Roman bobbed and weaved; peppering him with jabs as punches as they worked together, figuring out a battle plan for the upcoming fight.

Roman knew in his heart that he could beat Golkin. He just needed a workable plan, and the plan they came up with was to allow Golkin to gain confidence and show off in the first round, which he always liked to do. And then just when Golkin thought he had the fight in the bag, to open the throttles with the jab and begin to take command of the fight; punch by punch every round after that.

With a battle plan set, the men finished up their training at El Shacko and then made the move to their mountain training camp for the final four weeks of preparation till the fight. Once back in the mountains Roman, Gibby and Serby alternated between their workouts in the ring, their time on bicycles and running the trails, with some "recreational time" as Roman called it; by finding, cutting and splitting logs for their ever-growing reserve of stacked firewood that they would rely on to heat the cabin and barn when winter set in.

Roman had liked the work splitting and stacking firewood for his mountain cabin in Fairbanks, Alaska- and now years later, this time spent doing the same thing at Doc's mountain training camp gave him similar feelings of sweat-equity, satisfaction and preparation for the long winter ahead.

After Roman, Gibby, and Serby had all fallen asleep one night, Doc heard something going-on outside the cabin door, and woke them to share what was happening. (Earlier that afternoon, Gibby had put some stale bits of bread out on the picnic table to feed the birds). Now a mother raccoon had discovered the bread, and she was busy teaching her kits by example. One at a time they would scamper onto the table, and take a piece of bread down to the old cast iron sink -that was serving a new life as a bird bath- and dunk it in the water, before eating it. The raccoon family didn't even seem fazed when the men brought out a Coleman lantern to see the show better.

Roman went back to his room laughing, thinking about the raccoon family, and how it reminded him of the fun he and Antoinette had one time, while watching a squirrel outside their place in Fairbanks, try to carry an entire loaf of French bread across their front yard. Over and over the little squirrel had tumbled as it tried to run as fast as it could with its new found treasure. Memories of Antoinette giggling, and laughing away at the little creature's perseverance were still on his mind as he drifted back to sleep. He woke the next day feeling refreshed and still thinking about good times.

As the fight drew closer, Roman doubled his time and effort at climbing the very steepest sections of paved highway and dirt trails that led to the peaks near their mountain camp. Each hill in the area became a worthy opponent that he conquered over and over.

Then it was time. The men made the journey down the mountain and into the city of San Bernardino. And just like before, they arrived a day early to spend the night at the hotel, and be ready for weigh-in the next afternoon and at the auditorium for the scheduled ten-round exhibition fight at 8 p.m.

Golkin was not at the 2:00 p.m. Weigh-in when Roman stepped on the scale and tipped the bar at a muscular two hundred and fifty-four pounds. With six hours left until fight time the men drove back to the hotel to wait. At exactly 7:15 the men arrived at the Scribner Auditorium and went directly to the dressing room to make final preparations. Just as Doc finished carefully taping Roman's hands the door opened and a head popped in and said, "Fight time boys!"

Roman was the first to get to the ring and the cheering crowd remembered him as he climbed up onto the canvas and ducked between the ropes. Finally Golkin appeared and began his walk down the aisle and into the light of the boxing ring. The announcer made the introductions and again the crowd cheered as they heard, "...and fighting out of Fairbanks, Alaska... Roman Lefthanded Losinski."

Golkin eyed him silently, as the ref gave them last minute instructions and then told them to touch gloves, go to their corners, and come out fighting.

In the first fifteen seconds Golkin had tagged Roman with his left hand jab three times as Roman ducked-weaved-bobbed away from the onslaught. Just according to plan, Roman was letting Golkin take over the first part of the round and only offering an occasional jab in return. Golkin had in his eye the familiar glint of their previous fights. But he began to notice Roman was quicker and much better at ducking and covering and keeping himself away from the powerhouse punches Golkin was trying to set up. With ten seconds left in round one, Roman countered a Golkin jab with two lightning quick jabs of his own and a straight left punch on the nose just as the bell sounded for the end of round one.

So now the fight was on... Roman knew he had a fight on his hands, but he had put the question in Golkin's mind and now it was time to settle it. From the opening bell of round two each time Golkin tried to tag Roman with his left hand jab, he had to deal with a lightning quick right hand that Roman had figured out how to stick in his face, sometimes as gentle as a feather duster, and then the next time with the power of sledge hammer out of nowhere. The bell ending round two sounded and the men returned to their corners.

"Looking good Roman, looking good," Gibby offered as he sat down.

In round three Golkin got in a few well-placed jabs and tried to find an opening for his devastating right, but suffered each time in return, as Roman countered with punches and then just as quickly got out of range. This time Golkin was the one getting a boxing lesson, and his face was quickly beginning to show the damage-as a piece of fruit shows the bruises of rough treatment. And the skin covering his ribs was beginning to get a red glow from the pounding it was getting with the barrage of lefts and rights Roman was pounding into it. But he was a tough fighter and wasn't about to go down easy, until a right caught him across the bottom rib that felt like a red hot poker had been jammed into his heart, and a powerful left out of nowhere smashed into his jaw and sent him crashing butt-first to the canvas. He got up shaking his head, just as the bell sounded for the end of round three.

If there was a question in Golkin's mind before, now it had turned to outright confusion....

Round four brought on the meat of the battle. Each man jabbed and hammered away with fierce punches into the ribs and head of the other, and each searched for the right openings to land the combination of big punches to take the other man to the unconscious land.

At the end of round five Roman found that opening, and he threw a right-hand punch into a spot just under Golkin's ribs and connected with another left on the edge of his jaw. Down he went, but was again saved by the bell-signaling the end of round five.

As the bell sounded for the beginning of round six Roman

was the only fighter to stand up. Golkin was not able to answer the bell. The fans went wild as the ring announcer made the call and held up Roman's hand in victory.

It was all like in slow motion, his arm being raised up just like in the pre-fight visualizations Serby and he had practiced in the days leading up to the fight. So now he had finally beaten his old enemy Golkin, and done it convincingly by putting him on his butt two times in five rounds.

NINE

The Crowd Goes Wild

Back at El Shacko the men basked in celebration of the victory, took a few days off for recovery, and then back to the preparation for Roman's next fight. Again they spent the first three weeks in the desert followed by four weeks in the mountains. This time Roman's opponent was two hundred and fifty-eight pound Terry Stratton, who spent the first sixty-two seconds of round one trying to avoid being hit by an onslaught of punches before getting clocked with a left that put him down and out-cold on the canvas. The crowd, now soundly behind their Alaskan adoptee, went wild as Roman's hand was again held aloft for yet another victory. The big man from Alaska was quickly earning a reputation of being one tough fighter.

Doc arranged for the next fight to be held at the Perry Center in Los Angeles. Stories of Roman's previous victory's had been carried in the sports sections of newspapers across Southern California; and now a build-up of pre-fight publicity and posters that Doc and Bob Abrams had arranged ensured that fans would know where Roman was going to fight next.

The opponent chosen was Oscar Lopez a two hundred and

forty pound heavyweight with the experience of 27 professional fights. He had won 24, 22 by knockout. But when he got into the ring with Roman, he only lasted a minute and fifty-two seconds before being knocked out in the first round.

News reports of Roman's heavyweight battles we spreading fast, and were even carried by his adopted Alaskan hometown paper; the Fairbanks Daily News Miner. This big Alaskan fighter was gathering fans up and down the West Coast like a huge snow ball rolling down a snow covered hillside.

One by one, he began climbing the mountain of heavyweights that stood between him and his goal. Over the next eleven months, he scored first round knockouts of every single opponent that Doc and Bob Abrams could find to set him up against.

Then Doc, Bob Abrams and others, got the dangerous "Banjo Joe" Fulmer to sign a contract for a lop-sided percentage of the purse, if he would agree to fight Roman. Banjo Joe would get to keep 80% of the money and he figured Roman was inexperienced as a Pro anyway, and would be another easy mark. Banjo Joe was ranked as a number one contender for the heavyweight crown and was a veteran of 57 pro fights. He had won 52 fights, 48 by knockout. He had been trying to get a fight with the champ, but this deal was dropped into his lap first. It was good money, and besides it was all part of a deal worked out to guarantee him a title shot right after he dispatched the Newest-Johnny-Come-Lately, the upshot Roman Lefthanded Losinski.

The fight was set to be held at the MGM Grand Hotel in Las Vegas in just three months.

With the ink still drying on the contract, Roman and company headed off to the boxing camp at El Shacko. Doc was pulling it off. His expertise in contracts, and his old associates with the really big money in horse racing and gambling in Vegas, was the grease they needed for entry into the world of the big leagues-surrounding the contenders for the heavyweight crown.

TEN

Time for Reflection

Back at El Shacko the men carefully planned out the next thirteen weeks of training. They got every tape of Banjo Joe's fights, and analyzed his every punch. Gibby adopted Joe's style of vicious hooks to the head and body and threw every punch he could at Roman during their sparring sessions in the ring. Roman came up with a style of defense that included counter punching, ducking, blocking or simply leaning back away from, and thereby only absorbing a part of the force of the punches as he tried to minimize the potential damage of their impact.

Everyday Serby and Roman jogged up and down the sand trails to the bat caves. They practiced for hours the power of positive imaging, by holding the mental pictures of what they wanted to happen. And Roman often jogged along the trails solo late into the night as he visualized each round of the fight.... There were times when he was all alone on the trail, and he could feel Antoinette's positive presence all around him, as he ran across the sand. He could feel her love flowing over him, and filling him with energy along the path.

As the first three weeks in the desert drew to a close, the men decided to stick to their previous schedule of moving up to their mountain camp for their usual four weeks of training at high elevation. Running up and down the steep mountain-side trails and climbing the near-vertical paved summits on bicycles took on an increased level of importance, as they each sought the peak conditioning that would be required for the upcoming battle. They were in the big leagues now and the next battle Roman faced with Banjo Joe would be the tell-all of his conditioning and preparation, and a supreme test of all their hard work as a team.

Over and over they practiced the routine of their training schedule. Finally when the end of their four weeks in the mountains came, with seven weeks still remaining until the fight with Banjo Joe, Doc suggested they return directly to El Shacko and take a couple of days off from training. He hinted that perhaps now they could have the sailboat races that he and Roman had been kidding each other about since the first day Roman had seen Doc's two identical 12 foot Beetle Cat sailboats.

Doc came up with a plan where they could race as teams of two on each boat, and since he and Gibby together weighed about equal to the combined weight of Serby and Roman, the teams were set. Doc designed the course similar to the old Catboat races he had read about that were held off Cape Cod on the East Coast just after the turn of the last century. The last leg of the race course was designed for a down-wind section and was purposely close to the shoreline, the idea being that the 'crew' was supposed to jump off the boat and swim the short distance back to shore and leave the helmsman on board to steer the "lightened boat" for the final down-wind-dash to the finish line. Luckily the high salt content of the Salton Sea meant that crew members, Gibby and Serby, would float easily and find the short swim back to shore "a breeze," or so Doc assured them.

After a few practice sessions of the crew members jumping off the tiny boats and a lot of laughter, the teams were ready for the real race. The Grand Prize for the winners was to be a soak at the hot springs and a full dinner for all four of them at the El Toro Bravo Mexican Restaurant, with the bill being paid for by the losers.

Doc had set up a small marker buoy offshore about a quarter mile to the south of El Shacko, and declared that the course would begin on a start line by the end of the pier in-front of El Shacko, then go once around this south buoy, then head three-fourths of a mile north to Bob's Playa Riviera and once around the buoy outside the harbor, and then back as close as possible to the beach for the crew member jump-off point, and the final down-wind high-speed dash to the official finish at the end of the pier directly in-front of El Shacko.

On race day a stiff afternoon breeze guaranteed an exciting race, the team of Roman and Serby jumped to an early lead, and their boat was the first around buoy marker number one. On the up-wind leg Roman proved to be a skilled helmsman as he navigated the course and increased the lead to almost two boat lengths as they made the mark around the harbor buoy at Bob's Playa Riviera. Then as the two teams veered close to shoreline, Doc's partner Gibby dove off first and Serby followed, laughing as they did and each cheering their boat captains on for the final dash to the finish. The huge sails filled with air as the two boats skimmed along nearly side-by-side across the surface of the water. Doc's vessel surged forward and pulled even with Roman's boat, and then inching ahead, ever so slowly, finally claimed victory by "a mere whisker" as the two boats charged across the finish line.

That night at the hot springs the men all laughed together as they soaked in the warm waters, relaxing and kidding each other about the race, and possible future rematches.

Over dinner Doc raised his glass for a toast congratulating Roman and Serby for their valiant day's effort, and then turned to each of them as he thanked them personally for their Herculean efforts over the last year, and for bringing them all into the big leagues of heavyweight boxing. No matter what the outcome of the fight with Banjo Joe, they had each proven they were winners at what they did, and he was honored and proud to work and live with them.

Back at camp, the men continued their training. They lived in "day-tight compartments," or "fought one fight at a time," as Serby liked to refer to it when they focused only on the job at hand, and tailored their training specifically for each up-coming fighter's strengths and weaknesses. As he suggested, they looked forward to the upcoming fight as being "Their Payday" for all the hard work and effort. The days in the desert flashed-by, and then they made their move to the mountain camp for the last bit of training at altitude; where they would make their final preparations for the fight with Banjo Joe Fulmer.

Once they were settled back into their routine in the mountains, their bodies again began the process of adapting to the higher altitude and thinner air. The last four weeks of training at high altitude is what Doc felt was important to accomplish, and said would make the last bit of difference and boost Roman's endurance, especially for their next fight, thousands of feet lower in the desert community of Las Vegas.

After training all day long each day, Roman went right back to his "recreational time," cutting and splitting logs each evening until dark. He continued adding to the stacks of firewood until he was happy. He also selected and cut several seven-inch diameter logs into six-foot lengths, and would often carry one across his shoulders on training runs and then stop and do sit-ups with the big log resting across his arms and chest for extra weight.

He also began naming specific trees along the uphill sections of their running trails and bike routes "Old Joe," in reference to his next opponent, and would give extreme efforts up and down the hills in those sections; while running and riding the bike---just so he could smoke-past "Old Joe" in a dominating fashion.

Then it was time....

ELEVEN

A Guaranteed Title Shot

The four men made the five-hour drive to Las Vegas and checked into their rooms at the MGM Grand Hotel the day before the fight. At the weigh-in the next day, Banjo Joe Fulmer was there early- and the scale read two hundred and forty-eight pounds just before he stepped off. He stuck around to see what Roman weighed, and while he waited he leaned against the wall while strumming an old banjo and singing a little song he had made up to try and unnerve his newest opponent. "Step in the ring and dance with me Loser Losinski and you'll see stars and hear the music, just as the lights go out...."

Roman stepped onto the scale platform. Whatever the effect of Joe's behavior had on everyone else in the room, it didn't seem to bother Roman as he smiled over at Doc when the bar on the scale leveled-out and indicated two hundred and forty-six pounds of trim fighting weight.

The House was packed and the crowd cheered as the boxers climbed into the brightly lit ring that night. Joe was still mouthing the words to his song, as the referee gave the men the usual ring instructions. The men touched gloves and went to their corners to wait for the opening bell.

As if signaling fulfillment of a lifelong dream, Roman heard the bell and launched-out to the center of the ring.

Joe jumped straight on the offensive with three quick jabs and a right hook that just missed connecting with Roman's head. Roman peppered him with a couple of jabs and then backed out of range before Joe could throw a counter punch. The fans were going wild and sensed this was going to be a good fight between these two giant gladiators in the spotlight of the arena. Each man trying to sense the others style, and figure out a plan of attack. Joe was throwing power punches already- and each impact could be heard all the way into the seats at the back of the house. Roman was taking most of the blows on his huge forearms while he tried to move away from, and yet remain covered-up, and only occasionally did he try to defend himself with a quick jab as he tried to not leave any openings. Around the ring Joe pursued him, banging in three and four punches to every one Roman offered in return. Then finally the bell sounded, signaling the end of round one.

Round two began much the same way as Roman circled backwards and tried to remain just out of range, as he ducked and slipped as many punches as he could, while absorbing the damage from as few of the punches as possible; while sticking once-and-a-while and tossing in his own stiff jab in return and an occasional right-left-right combination. Round two ended with Roman throwing less than half the number of punches that Joe did. But the crowd seemed to sense that the big man from Alaska was absorbing the punishment for a reason and waiting for something.

In round three Roman began using the ropes wisely as he leaned back on them while absorbing the punches and then rolling away first to the right, and then the left, and dishing out his own jab, square into his opponents face, before quickly moving out of range; and then pausing for a second and allowing himself to be caught again against the ropes. Each time the punches into his sides and forearms could be heard, "Wham, wham, wham..." like a battering ram attacking the gates of a castle. Then he would roll off the ropes and sock in his lightning-quick jab and follow it with a stinging left. Round three ended with Roman only throwing about half as many punches as his opponent.

"I'm OK, I'm OK," he told his corner men, before smiling and adding, "I think I'm wearing him down."

Round four began with Roman countering his opponents' first punch with a quick flurry that showed he was still ready to tango. Again Roman seemed to relax back on the ropes, as his opponent went on the offensive with the left and right hooks slamming into Roman's sides and forearms. Roman sprung back away from the punches, and then spun off the ropes while adding in a jab to his opponents head and a left hook to the ribs, before quickly moving out of range. The training Roman and his team had done was paying off now, and he was just beginning to feel a second-wind as the bell signaling the end of round four sounded.

Right away at the beginning of round five Roman's opponent had him on the ropes again, and began throwing a continual barrage of haymakers that seemed likely to signal the end of the fight, but before the referee moved-in, Roman rolled away and opened up his own cannons. First a feather light right jab, then followed by another with the power of a sledgehammer, and then a left that snapped back the head of his opponent. Roman backed out and circled away, then just as quick back-in with a flurry of right-left-right combinations that went unanswered, while Joe tried to cover up. Then Roman saw the opening and threw a smoking right just below the bottom rib on Joe's left side, and a cannon ball left to the jaw that dropped Banjo Joe butt-first onto the canvas, and left him wondering what had hit him. He got up before the count of ten and seemed-to-the-referee to be ready to continue, but only survived the first five or six lightning quick sledgehammer-like punches from Roman before falling face-first onto the mat. He managed to struggle onto his knees but wasn't willing or able to get up before the count of ten.

The ring announcer held Roman's hand high and announced, "A victory by knock-out at one-minute and forty-nine seconds of round five...." as Roman looked out from under the lights and bowed his head slightly and basked in the applause of the cheering crowd.

That night over the victory dinner, Doc piped up with an announcement. "I don't know if you guys noticed the fine print clause that Joe negotiated for, that was finally added into the contract." The men all looked at him in surprise. "Well anyway," he continued. "Joe wanted a guarantee of getting a title shot with the champion after he beat you, and so Bob Abrams and a few of the other unnamed money people here in Vegas got the champ, Lester 'Bad Boy' Williams, to agree to it. So we put in the clause that, "The victor would claim first rights to a fight for the heavyweight crown with Lester 'Bad Boy' Williams." Not many people guessed that you could win Roman, but you did it, you whupped Banjo Joe Fulmer, and now we are set for a run at the heavyweight crown. The champ was sitting ring-side watching your fight, and Bob Abrams was ready with a contract in his pocket, and sitting right next to him. We got the champ to sign on the dotted line while the ring announcer was holding up your hand, and he wants the fight to be held at Harrah's Hotel and Casino in Lake Tahoe fourteen weeks from tonight."

Smiles broke-out all around the table and then Roman stood up. He rested a gentle hand on Serby's shoulder and said, "I have been dreaming of being 'A Contender' ever since I was a kid.

You three men, in making that dream possible; have made me the happiest man on earth. I thank you, and I am deeply indebted to all of you." And with that, he joyfully raised his glass in a toast to each of them, thanking them for believing in him and for investing their time, money and hard work....

TWELVE

You've always been my Champion...

With just fourteen weeks to prepare for the title fight, the men traveled back to the desert camp that had served them so well. After the Victory Celebration Party was over, they got down to business, and began the preparation necessary to get Roman ready for his fight with the champ.

As before, they got tapes of their upcoming opponents' previous fights, and together they analyzed his style and punching power. Roman and Serby covered some easy miles of jogging along the beach and across the sand trails for the first few days, to allow Roman's body to time to heal from the pounding it took while in the ring with Banjo Joe.

Gibby went back over every page of his 'Eat to Win Diet Plan' and made a new shopping list for re-supplying the shelves with the very freshest and best organic foods he could find. And Doc settled back into his relaxation-mode of stress relieving sailboat voyages along the coast of the Salton Sea.

Soon the men were right back into their early morning

routine of roadwork on the bikes, or long slow jogs, followed by a healthy breakfast, and then doing calisthenics, and ring work-outs till noon. Their afternoons were filled with more roadwork and jogging, and then back in the ring until dinner time. Roman was right back at it after dinner, going for long brisk walks, of jogging, and then pounding away at the heavy bag and speed bag, or skipping rope until late at night.

Day after day the men rehearsed their battle plans and trained following the same routines that had helped get them where they were. Roman fully realized he had made it to the big times, and these men, his friends, had helped him get there, His debt and sense of gratitude was enormous.

At night he often had dreams of Antoinette and felt her love empowering him as he went along his almost dream-like journey. Waking each morning with happy thoughts still on his mind, he got up from his bunk and greeted each new day, and each of his friends with his characteristic smile.

The habits and routines of their daily training became so engrained in them -that it became almost like breathing- and each felt a sense of emptiness or loss if they skipped or missed a long distance run, bike ride, or afternoon sparring session in the ring.

The clean desert air filled their lungs and fueled them, as they each grew stronger and healthier in their quest for peak performance. Then time remaining for this session in the desert evaporated, and it was time to move.

Pausing only for the three-hour drive to the mountains, the men were right back into their mountain-camp daily training routine. They would be training in the mountains again for four glorious weeks. As their training progressed, each man sensed the finely-honed polish of Roman's readiness, and yet each one fully realized and knew the dangers that could way-lay them, and each one knew they were training for what would probably one of the toughest opponents Roman had ever faced. Over and over, running up and down every hill and along every trail, they trained and ran on until it seemed like their lungs might burst or hearts explode, and still they ran on. Over each hill and down the other side, their lungs continued all the while to draw in the clean mountain air, and their hearts continuing to pump the oxygen-rich blood needed to sustain and nourish their lives. Each evening they welcomed their return to the cabin- and to the hot showers and lounged in the fancy tiled setting of the steam room. This was the way to train, and Doc made it all possible.

When they returned to El Shacko at the Salton Sea, they joked about having more sailboat races, but decided to postpone them until after the big fight. Again they jogged along the beaches, and up the sandy trails, building strength, power and endurance into their muscles, minds and hearts. Round after round his wise boxing trainers put him through the paces in the ring, and shared with him every last bit of knowledge they could remember that might help him in tough situations. Day after day and night after night Roman used every spare minute to soak-up their wisdom and improve his strength, skills, and readiness for the upcoming battle. Their time in the desert was coming to a close. Just before they left for the mountains, Serby and Roman took some time to paint the backgrounds and sketch the lettering for some of the signs Serby had been working on. "Are there any quotes on the list that you like better than the others?" Serby asked him.

"I like them all, but this one is my favorite," he said, pointing to the one Serby was working on.

GENERAL IDEAS FOR SUCCESS:

PREPARATION

PERSPIRATION

FOLLOW THROUGH

Once again, with just four weeks left until the fight, they made the move back up to the mountain camp for more training at high elevation. Roman again attacked every paved hill in the area on his fancy racing bike, like he was conquering some wild adversary. He climbed the steepest hills using the big chain-ring on the front sprocket, and as he churned the big gears, he prided himself that he saved the easier gears for emergencies, in-case he was having an off day, or felt sick. They jogged for hours and hours up and down every steep hillside in the area, and they practiced over and over their battle plans in systematic preparation for the fight with Lester Bad Boy Williams.

Then three days before the fight they boarded a specially chartered plane that Doc had arranged, and took a direct flight to Northern California, and landed on a small airstrip near Lake Tahoe. Doc had planned, that they arrive early, get a rental car, book into the hotel, and then take a couple of days off from training. "Just to relax," he said. The next morning, he suggested that they take a hike along Fallen Leaf Trail near Emerald Bay.

Following his suggestion, and getting away from all the people and the bustle of the Glitzy hotel, they made the forty-minute drive around the south end of the lake, past Emerald Bay to Fallen Leaf Campground. There they began the hike, and found themselves walking under giant Ponderosa Pine trees that towered over the trail and hillsides, and created a beautiful pine needle covered forest floor. The Clear mountain air, and the aroma from the pine trees, combined with a fine dust of the pulverized granite trail to give the whole area a beautiful clean earthy smell. The trail wound around the shoreline of a small lake that was hidden from the view of highway travelers, and was only accessible by hiking trails, or by travel on a small service road that went directly to five or six cabins that dotted the shoreline. Doc was right; hiking this trail around Fallen Leaf Lake was very relaxing. They meandered along the shoreline and eventually came upon a couple of avid trout fishermen that were tossing out bobbers-and-bait, and lures; in the hopes of landing one of the mysterious big lake trout that were reported to lurk in the deep clear-blue waters.

Farther up the trail, on a shady section of the pine-needle covered forest floor, they stopped to eat the lunch that Gibby had packed for the trip. While sitting under one of the tall pine trees, Roman decided it was the perfect time and place to take a nap. He stretched out flat and soon dozed off to sleep, and again dreamt about the happy times in his life, and mostly about Antoinette.

Serby and Gibby let him rest while they watched a mom and dad and a couple of kids pull stringers of beautiful pan-sized trout from the lake. It was late afternoon when they finally woke Roman, made the hike back to the car, and then drove back to the hotel. A fluffy cloud-covered sky over Lake Tahoe took on a beautiful yellow-hue, as golden rays streamed down from the afternoon sun, like spokes from some glorious wheel high above.

Reporters, Press Photographers, and handlers crowded into a packed room for the official weigh-in the next afternoon. Cameras flashed, reporters asked questions and took notes as Lester bad Boy Williams stepped onto the scale-registering two hundred and thirty-nine pounds of fierce fighting muscle, and spouting-off that he was going to demolish Roman in the early rounds and be playing Black Jack at the gaming tables before 9 p.m.

Lester and his crowd left the room before Roman even stepped onto the scale. The bar tipped and leveled out at two hundred and forty-three pounds as Roman smiled over at Doc. A camera flashed, and a reporter from Alaska covering the story for the Fairbanks Daily News Miner asked the question, "Roman with so few Professional fights under your belt, do you think you even have a chance?"

Roman responded, "We're here aren't we?"

In the privacy of the dressing room after Doc had carefully taped Roman's hands, and after Roman had warmed up by shadow boxing in front of the mirror, Doc presented him with a hand-tailored red silk robe designed especially for him and for this important event. Across the back of the robe in large hand-embroidered letters were the words, "THE CONTENDER."

At 8p.m. Roman and his team entered the hallway, and turned down the aisle leading to the center of the arena. The roar of the waiting crowd was enormous as Roman and his team made their way closer to the boxing ring.

Climbing onto the ring apron, and under the top rope, he looked out from under the lights, as the crowd applauded- and waited for Lester Bad Boy Williams to make his entrance. Down the aisle- and wearing a hooded black robe with lettering on the back that read: "BAD BOY..." Lester and his entourage finally came, accompanied by loud chants from the crowd, "Bad Boy, Bad Boy..."

Lester climbed into the ring and the noise from the crowd was deafening. Minutes later, when the crowd finally quieted down, the ring announcer grabbed the microphone and made his call, "Fighting out of this corner, the challenger, from Fairbanks, Alaska, Roman Lefthanded Losinski, and fighting out of this corner, from Los Angeles, California, The Heavyweight Champion of the World, Lester Bad Boy Williams!"

The two men came to the middle of the ring, and the

referee gave them their instructions and then told them to touch gloves, return to their corners, and come out fighting.

The bell rang. The men met in the center of the ring, and the champ went directly on the offensive and pounded two quick jabs into the challengers face. Roman tossed back a jab of his own and then circled backwards as the champ pursed and pounded in a hook to the ribs and a right to the head. The crowd cheered loudly.

"This guy can hit!" ---Roman thought, as he tried to find space and time in the ring to focus his thoughts. "...keep your guard up, make him miss when you can- and begin peppering him with jabs, adding in a few stingers now and then to assume control..." he thought to himself. Lester advanced and banged in a left and then a straight right to the head. The crowd was going wild! Roman blocked the next punch and returned two quick jabs, and backed out of range. Lester followed and whacked in a couple of hooks into Roman's ribs that the challenger was able to partially block with his arms. Moving quickly to the left and then back to the right Roman tried to confuse and frustrate Lester. He was having none of it, and connected with a jab and then three power punches into Roman's side. The challenger circled backwards, stopped then smacked in a jab and then hammered a straight left to Lester's jaw. "There, have a taste of your own!" Roman thought. "This guy isn't that hard to hit. I just have to slip the punches, and remember to duck and jab... duck and jab," thinking back to the wise words his trainers had used so often.

After getting over being 'psyched-out' early in the fight, and then figuring out that he could hit this guy, Roman got down to business, and began the process of trading punches and staying covered as best as he could. Round one seemed like it was taking forever as he punched, and got punched-back in return it seemed about twice as many times. The crowd was soundly behind the champ, and cheered loudly any time it seemed-like he threw a damaging punch, and that egged-on Lester in pursuit, as he swung in punch after punch, hoping to end this thing. But Roman had trained hard for this fight, and he had come here prepared, knowing full well he would have to take some damage, and do his best to give plenty back in return.

Then out of nowhere he felt the concussion and everything went black. Punches continued to slam into his head and ears. He slumped to the canvas, and when he looked up the referee was standing over him and counting, "...two...three...four..." Roman looked around for the eyes of his corner-men, but he was facing the wrong direction, "five...six...seven..." Then he heard her voice softly in his ears, "Get up Roman, get up...hurry!" On the count of eight he was on his feet, and the referee looked into his eyes- and then motioned the other man in. Lester swooped in to finish him off, looking for the perfect opening.

Roman thought, "Hook your arms around him and tangle him up." Lester's swinging arms were ineffective as the challenger brought his arms around him and squeezed the mass together. Lester slipped free and pounded in two more punches and Roman instinctively hammered back two straight rights into Lester's jaw, just as the bell sounded, signaling the end of round one.

In his corner, his team massaged his legs and shoulders and did everything they could, as they tried to help him recover. He used every second of the rest between rounds, as he let his muscles relax, and accepted a mouthful of water from the squeeze bottle Serby was holding; spit it back into the funnel, and then accepted half-a-mouthful more and swallowed it.

The time between rounds passes quickly, but to a well-conditioned boxer it can be just what he needs to make a significant recovery. "Use the whole ring to stay away from him Roman, and use your lightning speed to poke the jab in his face, and keep him off balance," were the last words he heard his corner-men say, before the bell rang- and he launched out to the center of the ring.

Round two began and Lester tried to force the pace and get Roman to make a mistake. But Roman was having none of it, and he worked the ring like an old-time pro, making Lester chase him around the ring. Roman relied on the footwork that Gibby had taught him, and the months and months of aerobic conditioning that Serby had coached him on, and the years of physical strength built-in from working hard as a laborer, to make a complete recovery before the end of the round. Before the bell sounded he was beginning to score points with his lightning quick jab. Lester still pursued and managed to tag him with jabs, but every time Lester got in position to swing a haymaker he got knocked off-balance by a jab he never saw coming, and then Roman danced back out of the way. Round two ended. Lester was now ahead on points on all score cards in rounds one and two. But Roman had survived round two, and had now---fully recovered.

At the start of round three Roman banged out three quick jabs in the face of the champ, then followed them with a straight left, and for the first time he even heard a small group in the crowd cheer for him. Lester circled in and connected with a jab and two hooks before Roman moved out of range. Over the course of the next two and a half minutes the two gladiators traded punches that would have knocked out lesser opponents. Jab followed jab as the two men alternately stood their position and swung punches, and then ducked or backed out to avoid being damaged by dangerous counter punches.

By the conclusion of round three, more fans in the crowd were soundly behind Roman, since he had earned their respect for his courage, his dogged determination, his ability to take a punch, and his impressive display of boxing skills. As round three ended, the judge's score cards showed that he was just slightly behind on points for that round. But the tide was changing.

At the opening bell of round four, Lester hammered in two quick jabs and tried to follow them with a left, but it missed, Roman capitalized on it with a right-left-right combination, and then circled out of range. Then he spun back in and tagged Lester with a solid jab, and a left hook and two more unanswered rights. Roman danced back around the ring. He made Lester pursue him. Lester tried to connect with a jab and missed and took the punishment of another right-left-right combination from Roman. The challenger was getting his rhythm now and the crowd sensed it. The two men continued to trade punches, but Lester was getting the worst of it. Each time Roman would stick and jab and then see an opening and throw a hook, or a straight left, he could tell the punches were having their effect. When round four ended, for the first time in the fight, Roman had won a round on all score cards.

Round five began with Roman connecting with two jabs and a left hook that snapped Lester's head to the side. The champ covered up for a second and then went right back to his dogged pursuit of the challenger. Roman peppered him with a right, a left and two more rights and circled back out of range. Lester came at him with thunderous lefts and rights. Some connected and some missed. Roman absorbed the blows that connected and capitalized on the missed punches with jabs that flashed-in and lefts that smashed into the champs' cheek bones, eyes and temple. Roman was able to tag him now almost at will. Now it was the time to settle in for the long haul, and to keep scoring all the point-earning combinations that he could. This round was Roman's and he could sense it, and the crowd began cheering each time he stopped Lester in his tracks with a sledgehammer-like jab, or a left hook to the head, or body of the aggressor. The bell signaling the end of round five sounded.

In his corner Gibby rubbed his shoulders, and Serby told Roman that he was ahead on points in both rounds four and five, but to be careful, and watch for openings right after Lester throws the left hook.

"This guy is known for never quitting, and is always dangerous! Use the ring." Gibby advised him. "Stick and jab...stick and jab."

The bell sounded for the beginning of round six and Roman leapt off the corner stool and the two men met in the center of the ring. Lester got off a jab that connected and took two from Roman in return. Both men now were covered and dripping in sweat as they got into the rhythm for the long haul. This guy was no push-over, but neither was Roman. Lester was already late for "his appointment at the gaming tables," and Roman didn't plan to let him off---anytime soon.

Round six wore-on as each man gave, or absorbed, power punches to the body and head. Punches that each man knew would produce a knock-out, and had been enough to knock-out other men they had fought. But these two were different from other men, they were gladiators, and they were fighting for the glory of being the Heavyweight Champion of the World. It was Lester's Crown to lose, and Roman's to gain, if he could stay safe, uninjured- and just do it! Pacing himself carefully, and utilizing the constant irritant of his lightning-fast jab, and following it up with punishing combinations, and then moving out of harms-way so quickly that Lester had to constantly chase him; was a battle plan that was working out well. Roman was again ahead on points when the bell sounded for the end of round six.

Round seven began with Lester fully realizing he needed to do something to change the way this fight was going, especially after hearing the news loud-and-clear from his corner-men. He began putting everything he had in every punch, and each one was a haymaker. The punches that connected could be heard in the back seats of the arena, as they whammed into Roman's sides and head. Lester couldn't keep this pace up forever, and Roman knew it, and so he waited patiently, as a cat waits outside the hole of a mouse. Roman used his massive forearms and elbows as shields to absorb most of the power of the punches when he could, and then when he could see openings, he hammered back power punches of his own into the body, sides, and head of his aggressor.

Then just as Serby had described, Roman began to see openings each time Lester threw his left hook. There it was… a perfect opening for the punch Serby had described in detail, months earlier to Roman. Almost like in slow motion; Roman saw the perfect spot for that punch, there it was, right below Lester's bottom rib. In flashed Roman's right as he imagined his fist was a burning-hot three-inch round bar of solid steel, burning a hole up- and through Lester's heart and all the way to his backbone, and then adding in a lightning-quick power-house left to the bottom of Lester's jaw; dropped him like a sack of potatoes, precisely the same second that the end of round seven bell sounded. Roman spun and went to his corner, as Lester got up slowly, and staggered to his corner as his handlers helped onto the stool.

Lester recovered, but as round eight began, Roman could see a clear difference in Lester's eyes. He had fully earned Lester's respect. Lester was in top condition though, and the time between rounds had allowed him to make a rapid recovery. For a moment or two he was considerably less aggressive in his pursuit of Roman, and though he still tossed in his left hook, he quickly spun back away to the right and tried to keep clear of Roman's powerful weapon. Each man was now respectful of the power the other possessed. The battle raged on with flourishes first by one fighter- and then by the other. Before the end of the round, Lester was once again the main aggressor, but Roman was connecting more often and had again scored the majority of points on all score cards.

Between rounds Lester again was told by his corner men that he had to get with the program if he expected to win this fight. So once again he started off the round with all of his power in every punch. And as Roman had found-out, this guy could punch. Roman again effectively blocked -as many punches as he could with his forearms and elbows- and waited patiently for Lester to slow down or make a mistake and leave another big opening. That opening came right before the end of round nine. Again there was Lester's left hook, and the opening right there by the bottom rib. In went Roman's right arm like a red-hot poker right through his aggressors' heart- and then instantly just as Lester tried to suck backward away from the painful punch to the mid-section, he flinched his head forward, and collided with the left hand that Roman was powerfully aiming for the button on his opponents jaw. A loud crack was heard. Lester crumpled to the canvas, the bell rang. Lester again struggled up and onto his corner stool.

Again Lester made a recovery during the break between rounds. This time the two met in the center of the ring for round ten, eyeing each other, and looking to throw the powerhouse punch to take the other man out. Roman tagged Lester with the right jab consistently, but failed to follow it up with his combination left-right-left, and when he did: Doc saw him winch in pain. Lester saw it too! Sensing he was injured, Lester began pursuing Roman around the ring like before, and was whamming in damaging body shots. This time Roman was not so good at blocking them on his left side, and he tried to turn Lester away from that side. Lester immediately sensed an advantage and hammered away as many body punches as he could into Roman's weaker side. Roman would try to hold Lester away from it with a straight left punch, but it clearly had little effect in keeping Lester back. The round went on with Roman using his right arm for both the jab- and now his only means of defense. Lester gained confidence, as he began hammering in punches almost at will. Roman was losing this round, and he was taking a severe beating. He was not about to give-up though, and fought every second of the round courageously. Then the bell for round ten sounded.

In the corner Roman's team asked him, "What's wrong? Why aren't you using your left?" he held up his left glove, and almost in a guttural voice answered, "Hand broken..."

Doc suggested that they throw in the towel and end the fight, but Roman turned his head and stared at Doc.

"Don't you do it!" is all Roman said, before the bell for the start of round eleven sounded, and he got up off the stool and went out into the center of the ring.

The round began with Lester again on the pursuit, hunting Roman down. He smelled victory, and his punches were slamming-home into Roman's ribs and stomach. Roman began to try and throw his left -as best as he could- to keep Lester away from that side, and would spin away from Lester and punch back with his still powerful, but now growing weary-right hand. Roman's left side began to glow red, with the continual barrage of pounding it was taking. People at ringside could visibly see the swelling, as his rib-cage began to take on a misshapen look-almost like a pillow case stuffed with lumpy foam.

Lester knew he was close to victory, and that his punches were taking their toll---but every time he thought he almost had it won, Roman would swing and connect with a solid right, or a weakened left-right combination that would halt Lester in his tracks.

When the bell, signaling the end of round eleven sounded

Lester was ahead on all score cards for that round. He was now ahead on score cards for five rounds, but Roman had won rounds 4, 5,6,7,8, and 9 for a total of six rounds. Roman desperately needed to win the last round, or the fight would probably be decided in Lester's favor.

Between rounds, while his corner-men massaged his shoulders and legs, and then worked the muscles in his right arm, Roman suddenly got an idea. He winked over at Gibby, just as they heard the bell signaling the beginning of the twelfth round---the last round of the fight.

The two fighters stood up and approached each other; met in the middle of the ring, and touched gloves in a gesture of respect. Each man was searching deep inside himself for the strength to finish. Both fighters knew the importance of this last round. Lester needed to at least win this round, or knock Roman out to win the fight. Roman needed to win the round soundly for his only chance at victory. The big difference in the fight now, was that Roman had changed his stance and was now fighting as a right-hander. He was using the Detroit Gladiator Style that Gibby and he had worked on together, during their months of sparring sessions in the ring. It was working. Every time Lester got close enough to swing in a hook towards Roman's left side, he got a quick flash of Roman's left jab in his eyes, and then a thunderous right crashed into his face, knocking him off balance. Lester at first seemed confused and frustrated during the first part of the round, but then he began to get into a rhythm, and was soon back to pursuing Roman relentlessly around the ring. Lester was adding up more points as he pounded in more jabs and followed them with more point scoring combinations....

The round wore on. Roman was doing damage when he could, and waiting for the right opportunity. Lester continued the pursuit, and steadily added up points with his punches. Flurry after flurry, and punch after punch he racked up a commanding lead. Roman took the pounding and then, with less than-a-minute-left before the end of the fight, Lester threw in a flurry of unanswered punches, and finished them off with two more punishing left hooks... Time stopped... Roman saw the hooks coming, first one then the other. Wham! Wham! ---But he didn't feel them--- because there was the opening! The opening that Roman had been waiting for... In an instant, Roman swung in his right-hand with every bit of his power...power like the force of an I-beam falling twenty stories and crashing into the ground, smashing it into the same spot Roman had aimed for before, right below the bottom rib in Lester's mid-section. Roman saw it all happening, as if, like-in-slow motion. Lester froze, and in flashed the first punch... then Roman recoiled his right arm...and pounded it in again...and again, each time jamming it past the solar-plexus and up into Lester's spine. Then he topped it off with a blinding left jab, and followed with three pile-driver-like overhand rights in a row, Bam! Bam! Bam! -crashing them into the end of Lester's jaw. Lester dropped to the canvas. Lying in a heap, right in front of Roman's corner, he was barely moving. The referee ordered Roman to a neutral corner.

The referee stood over Lester and began the count. "One... two... three... four," he called out loudly. Roman looked across the ring and into the eyes of his team. They saw him wink at them. There he stood, his tired arms resting across the top of the upper ropes. Then he looked down at the floor by his feet- and sat down on the canvas to rest. He waited...leaning to one side, and supporting himself upright with his right arm. The referee continued his count while standing over Lester, "Five... six... seven..." The crowd was going wild!

Roman turned his eyes up into the glare of the overhead lights... "Is that you Antoinette?" he asked, looking into the bright light.

The referee's count continued, "Eight... nine... ten," The referee motioned---fight over...just seconds before the bell sounded, signaling the end of the final round...and end of the fight!

Roman turned his head and eyes back down to activity in the ring, and then looking just outside the ropes, his eyes met the eyes of his teammates. All three of them were shouting, smiling and jumping up and down. He smiled at them... one last time- and then slowly slumped over. A Ring Doctor got into the ring to check on the hurt-and-groggy Lester...After seeing that Lester was coming back to consciousness, the Ring Doctor turned his head back to look in Roman's direction. All eyes were now on Roman. The Ring Doctor went over to him. He bent down on one knee, put a stethoscope to Roman's heart- and then looked into his eyes.

Then he just stood-up, staring into the crowd, shaking his head---No!

-Then as if in a dream, Roman saw Antoinette, just outside the ring, she motioned for him to come to her. She was all dressed-up in a beautiful white dress. He climbed out of the ring and walked towards her. He looked back in the direction of his team and pointed to her -as if to show them how pretty she was- but they weren't watching him. They were just staring into the ring; at two fighters lying on the canvas, one of them wasn't moving. As Roman got closer to Antoinette... he realized what was happening... and so once more, with his characteristic smile on his face, he scooped her up in his arms, carried her up the aisle, and they left the building---Leaving a Ring full of confusion behind them....

###

We sincerely hope you enjoyed reading the book Champion A Story of the Happy Life of Roman Lefthanded Losinski. We also hope that if you found reading the story to be a good experience, that you will consider spreading the word about our book… and that you will encourage others to read Champion as well. We would be further delighted and honored, if you would consider writing a short one-sentence blurb/review, or even a longer review if you so desire, on Amazon or any of the Online bookstores that are kind enough to share both our print and eBook and Audiobook editions of Champion with readers around the world.

If you wish to find out more about the author Miles Cobbett, you can easily find more information via a quick google search, or other online search engine for: [Miles Cobbett] The results of your search will lead you to various Blogs, Interviews and multiple web pages full of information; including his Facebook pages, a LinkedIn page, and a twitter page, (@AlaskaMiles). You are welcome to contact him on any of those places if you have questions or comments, and please remember to let us know if you wish to be included on a mailing list for updates about future book releases.

(Here is one "Cool Reading Report" form that kids seem to enjoy sharing with their parents and teachers)

Name:

Date:

Grade:

Class/Teacher:

The name of the book I read was:

The author or editor was:

The story was basically about:

Three or four fun or interesting things I learned from reading this are:

One:

Two:

Three:

Four:

Signature:

(This is your chance to certify, place your signature, code-of-honor that you really read the book)

Champion by Miles Cobbett

A Story of the Happy Life of Roman Lefthanded Losinski

(Back cover)

"Roman Lefthanded Losinski – that's the name of a Boxer!" said an Alaskan writer feeling like he had 'just struck the pay dirt" of a marvelous idea.

"It is?" Well I've never heard of him!" said a friend.

"In my new book it is!" replied the author.

Five days later the author Miles Cobbett brought a semi-polished draft of Chapter One, to share with friends at a favorite cafe. Encouraged by their positive responses, and by their requests for more of the story, he continued to work on the rest of the book during daylight hours; and worked to pay the bills by shuttling passengers to-and-from the Fairbanks Airport as a night-time cab driver. Then he hired OfficeMax to handle the job of printing multiple copies for his own "Test Marketing Program." Over the next fourteen months he personally handed out over 3,000 copies or either the first chapter, or the first three chapters of his book to Alaskan travelers, friends, neighbors and acquaintances. The positive response from readers of all ages was enormous. Read a sample of what some of those readers of Champion had to say:

"Thank you very much for your story, I liked it a lot!" said a nine year old reader.

"I liked the part where Roman knocks the mean guy down," said another young reader.

"Wow that was great reading. What happens next?" replied a reader via email.

"I liked Roman. When can I get more chapters?" said Susan George from Juneau, Alaska.

"We loved your story. When can we get more?" said a previous shuttle-taxi customer at the Fairbanks Airport.

"Man I read your manuscript. It was great! I want to read more, when is the book coming out?" said another returning passenger at the airport.

"I was reading the story and I forgot where I was sitting, and didn't notice the sounds around me. I was in the story. This guy that's got something, but doesn't know it! It's just a neat story really. He stumbles into fame with his homegrown ability. It really put my imagination to work and it fascinated me, even though I didn't really care about boxing." said Wisconsin photographer Andrew Fritz

Another reader gave the following written reply to the author:

"The mark of a good writer is his ability to form complete pictures in the mind of his readers. The mark of a terrific writer is his ability to form emotions in the heart of the reader. You are performing both tasks in this, while building goals + challenges for the primary character. These first three chapters captured me." - Cessna pilot Robert Grediagin

Another reader wrote the following email response:

"Talking with you at Deb's cafe in Fairbanks & reading your 15 pages of Champion was really interesting. Your method of crafting your words to paper to draw pictures in the readers mind is a real talent! Your life of working at so many jobs allows you the down to earth understanding of the common man's struggles of everyday life. Your quick precise mind (of minor details), allows a clear and picture ability to the reader of your story! I'm looking forward to your Booksssssssss! I have given your handout to my wife, she hasn't read it yet but I am sure she will enjoy it. Looking forward to seeing you again and reading your books! Don't let anything stand in your way; follow your dream & ability! You're a winner. Send your scripts to Hollywood it will be your Gold Mine in life."

-Trucker, Glen

***

Dedication

To my (deceased) Mother, Vera who nurtured my reading habits as a child, and also taught me the value of a job done well. I fondly look back on the many valuable lessons I learned from her. Now as an adult, I look back and especially value her parental example of a strong will, and unwavering insistence, that I, (as a less-than-willing teenager) mow our lawn from three different directions and rake the entire lawn-thoroughly each time.

To my (deceased) Father Bryan, who taught me how to take things apart; and to examine how they worked, and why they worked, and to figure out how to make improvements on the original designs. Later he shared some of his knowledge and skills on building-and-tuning High Performance Racing Engines; and he allowed me to gain some early hands-on experience. I cherish the memories of his patient and gentle way of listening to my latest ideas. And I thank him for his example of putting his creative thoughts on paper, and for his encouragement of my own attempts at creative writing.

To my three older brothers: John, Raymond and Geoffrey for their guidance, and caring attitudes, and shared wisdom during my childhood: Including, teaching me a valuable life lesson about the inner-cowardly nature of bully's. And for the two dollars they dug out of their teenage pockets, in "Real silver quarters and dimes," and then put on the table, and told me –their crying five year old little brother- that I could have it all; if I first went outside and finished the fight with our neighborhood bully. So I re-entered the battle of flying fists and blood, and several minutes later won the fight; and sent the bully home crying and covered in blood; (mostly my blood, from a first-round bite to the thumb and wrist of my right hand), then I went back inside to collect my money.

To my friends… your help, encouragement, and friendship have meant the world to me. I will always cherish our good times together, and I wish for you all: Health, Happiness, and Prosperity.

And to the authors of books I have read authors that humble me, and inspire me with their skills and abilities as writers, but most importantly helped my enjoyment of reading and writing through the clarity and magnetism of their works for fiction, or through their well-reasoned arguments, their evocative ideas, and their keen sharpness of wit. In this last group I would like to single out three of my favorite books and their authors:

One, I would like to thank David Mamet for his thoughtful book, TRUE AND FALSE *** Heresy and Common Sense for the Common Actor. (I read his book and searched for ways to apply his ideas to the craft of writing.).

Two, I would like to thank Jennifer Lerch for her invaluable book, 500 Ways to Beat the Hollywood Script Reader *** Writing the Screenplay the Reader will Recommend. (I used Jennifer's book first as a guidebook and later as a launching pad for my "Test Marketing Program").

Three, I would like to thank David Lambuth, "And Others," for their witty, clear and informative little book, The Golden Book 'On Writing.'

And last, but most importantly, I would like to thank you, the reading audience of Champion. Remember, You are the True Champions in Life.

Sincerely, Miles Cobbett

Who would like to read more about books by Miles Cobbett?

http://MilesCobbett.com

Miles Cobbett

ABOUT THE AUTHOR

The author left Seattle, Washington on a ship bound for Alaska, in the spring of 1982. He had; seven hundred dollars in his pocket, a duffle bag full of rugged work clothes, a portable typewriter-filled with paper, and a supply of steno-note pads and pens. He came looking for; story and character ideas and a way of making enough money to keep a roof over his head, and food in his belly. He found plenty of everything. Now twenty five years later, he is willing to share his stories with anyone who likes to read... See Miles Cobbett's webpage www.MilesCobbett.com

Miles Cobbett on Facebook

@AlaskaMiles on Twitter

Email: Alaskamiles@Yahoo.com

Made in the USA
Monee, IL
20 June 2021